More Praise for Han Kang's

The Vegetarian

"Ferocious . . . [Han Kang] has been rightfully celebrated as a visionary in South Korea. . . . Han's glorious treatments of agency, personal choice, submission, and subversion find form in the parable. . . . Ultimately, though, how could we not go back to Kafka? More than *The Metamorphosis*, Kafka's journals and 'A Hunger Artist' haunt this text."

—Porochista Khakpour, *New York Times Book Review*

"Astonishing . . . Kang viscerally explores the limits of what a human brain and body can endure, and the strange beauty that can be found in even the most extreme forms of renunciation."

—*Entertainment Weekly*

"A short novel of sexuality and madness that deserves its great success."

—Ian McEwan, EW.com

"Sometimes how a book or a film puzzles you—how it may mystify even its own creator—is the main point. The way it keeps slithering out of your grasp. The way it chats with you in the parlor even as it drags something nameless and heavy through the woods out back . . . That's the spirit in which to approach *The Vegetarian*. . . . *The Vegetarian* has an eerie universality that gets under your skin and stays put irrespective of nation or gender."

—Laura Miller, Slate.com

"It takes a gifted storyteller to get you feeling ill at ease in your own body. Yet Han Kang often set me squirming with her first novel in English, at once claustrophobic and transcendent."

—*Chicago Tribune*

"Provocative . . . shocking."
—*Washington Post*

"This is a deceptive novel, its canvas much larger than the mild social satire that one initially imagines. Kang has bigger issues to raise. . . . The matter of female autonomy assumes urgency and poignancy."
—*Boston Globe*

"Compelling . . . a seamless union of the visceral and the surreal."
—*Los Angeles Review of Books*

"Indebted to Kafka, this story of a South Korean woman's radical transformation, which begins after she forsakes meat, will have you reading with your hand over your mouth in shock."
—*O, The Oprah Magazine*

"If you love books that grab you by the throat and keep you wide-eyed and shocked throughout, you've got to pick up Han Kang's *The Vegetarian*."
—EW.com

"A complex, terrifying look at how seemingly simple decisions can affect multiple lives . . . In a world where women's bodies are constantly under scrutiny, the protagonist's desire to disappear inside of herself feels scarily familiar."
—VanityFair.com

"A sharply written allegory that extends far beyond its surreal premise to unexpected depths."
—*The Millions*

"An elegant tale."
—*Huffington Post*

"This elegant-yet-twisted horror story is all about power and its relationship with identity. It's chilling in the best ways, so buckle in and turn down the lights."
—Elle.com

"*The Vegetarian* is the first—there will be more, let's hope—of Han Kang's novels to arrive in the United States. . . . The style is realistic and psychological, and denies us the comfort that might be wrung from a fairy tale or a myth of metamorphosis. We all like to read about girls swapping their fish tails for legs or their unwrinkled arms for branches, but—at the risk of stating the obvious—a person cannot become a potted bit of green foodstuff. That Yeong-hye seems not to know this makes her dangerous, and doomed."
—*Harper's*

"This haunting, original tale explores the eros, isolation and outer limits of a gripping metamorphosis that happens in plain sight. . . . A remarkable novel."
—*Minneapolis Star Tribune*

"Complex and strange . . . This is a book that will stay with you."
—*St. Louis Post-Dispatch*

"Brutally yet beautifully explores the gap between one person's expression and another's reception."
—*Harvard Crimson*

"*The Vegetarian* is incredibly fresh and gripping."
—*The Rumpus*

"Disquieting, thought-provoking and precisely informed."
—*Shelf Awareness*

"Brilliant . . . an ingenious, upsetting, and unforgettable novel."
—*Publishers Weekly* (starred review)

"A spare, spectacular novel . . . Fans of authors as diverse as Mary Karr and Haruki Murakami won't be able to turn away."
—*Library Journal* (starred review)

"Elegant yet unsettling . . . Readers will want more of the author's shocking portrayals of our innermost doubts, beliefs, and longings."
—*Booklist*

"Beautiful and disquieting."
—*BookPage*

"An unusual and mesmerizing novel, gracefully written and deeply disturbing."
—*Kirkus Reviews*

"*The Vegetarian* is one of *the best* novels I've read in years. It's incredible, daring, and stunningly moving. I loved it."
—Laura van den Berg, author of *Find Me*

"If it's true you are what you read, prepare to be sliced and severed, painted and slapped and fondled and broken to bits, left shocked and reeling on the other side of this stunning, dark star of a book."
—Amelia Gray, author of *Gutshot*

"Searing . . . [Yeong-hye's] extreme efforts to separate herself from her animal appetites reveal the sanity and normality of those closest to her to be mere matchstick houses."
—Helen Oyeyemi, author of *Boy, Snow, Bird*

"Suffused with a sensibility that evokes the matter-of-fact surrealism of Franz Kafka, featuring a female protagonist as engagingly perverse as Melville's Bartleby . . . hypnotic, erotic, disquieting, and wise."
—James Morrow, author of *Galápagos Regained*

"A strange, painfully tender exploration of the brutality of desire indulged and the fatality of desire ignored, rendered all the more so by Deborah Smith's exquisite translation."

—Eimear McBride, Baileys Women's Prize for Fiction–winning author of *A Girl Is a Half-formed Thing*

"Visceral and terrifying, *The Vegetarian* is a startling reminder of the utter unknowability of another's mind. It is artfully plotted yet reads like a fever dream, sweeping and surreal. It will leave you aching."

—Sarah Gerard, author of *Binary Star*

"Like a small seed, Han Kang's startling and unforgettable debut goes to work quietly, but insistently. Her prose is so balanced, so elegant and assured, you might overlook the depths of this novel's darkness—do so at your own peril."

—Colin Winnette, author of *Haints Stay* and *Coyote*

"*The Vegetarian* is a story about metamorphosis, rage, and the desire for another sort of life. It is written in cool, still, poetic but matter-of-fact short sentences, translated luminously by Deborah Smith, who is obviously a genius."

—Deborah Levy, author of *The Unloved* and *Swimming Home*

"*The Vegetarian* is hypnotically strange, sad, beautiful, and compelling. I liked it immensely."

—Nathan Filer, 2013 Costa First Novel Award–winning author of *The Shock of the Fall*

"A stunning and beautifully haunting novel. It seems in places as if the very words on the page are photosynthesizing. I loved this graceful, vivid book."

—Jess Richards, Costa First Novel Award short-listed author of *Snake Ropes*

"Poetic and beguiling, and translated with tremendous elegance, *The Vegetarian* exhilarates and disturbs."
    —Chloe Aridjis, author of *Book of Clouds*

"Surreal and spellbinding."
    —Arifa Akbar, *The Independent*

"This short novel is one of the most startling I have read."
    —Julia Pascal, *The Independent*

"Immediately absorbing . . . The different perspectives offered are so beautifully distinctive. . . . Every word matters."
    —*Sunday Herald*

"A work of savage beauty and unnerving physicality."
    —*Irish Times*

"*The Vegetarian* whispers so clearly, it can be heard across the room, insistently and with devastating, quiet violence."
    —Joanna Walsh, *New Statesman*

"A strange and ethereal fable."
    —*Times Literary Supplement*

The Vegetarian

The Vegetarian

A Novel

HOGARTH
London / New York

Han Kang

Translated from the Korean by Deborah Smith

English translation copyright © 2015 by Deborah Smith

Copyright © 2007 by Han Kang

Excerpt from *Human Acts* by Han Kang, translation copyright © 2016 by Deborah Smith

Published in the United States by Hogarth, an imprint of the Crown Publishing Group, a division of Penguin Random House LLC, New York.
crownpublishing.com

HOGARTH is a trademark of the Random House Group Limited, and the H colophon is a trademark of Penguin Random House LLC.

This book was originally published in Korean as three separate novelettes and then compiled into a novel, 채식주의자 (*Ch'aesikjuuija*), published in 2007 by Changbi Publishers, Inc. Copyright © 2007 by Han Kang. This translation originally published, in somewhat different form, in Great Britain by Portobello Books, London, and subsequently published in hardcover in the United States by Hogarth, an imprint of the Crown Publishing Group, a division of Penguin Random House LLC, New York, in 2016. This edition is published by arrangement with Portobello Books.

This book contains an excerpt from the forthcoming book *Human Acts* by Han Kang. This excerpt has been set for this edition only and may not reflect the final content of the forthcoming edition.

Library of Congress Cataloging-in-Publication Data
Han Kang, 1970–
  [Ch'aesikchuuija. English]
  The vegetarian : a novel / Han Kang; translated from the Korean by Deborah Smith.
    pages cm
  I. Title.
  PL992.26.K36C4313 2015
  895.73'5—dc23

                         2015002206

ISBN 978-1-101-90611-8
eBook ISBN 978-0-553-44819-1

Printed in the United States of America

Book design by Lauren Dong
Cover design by Christopher Brand
Cover photograph by 100/Moment/Getty Images

10 9 8 7 6 5 4 3 2

First United States Paperback Edition

The Vegetarian

The Vegetarian

Before my wife turned vegetarian, I'd always thought of her as completely unremarkable in every way. To be frank, the first time I met her I wasn't even attracted to her. Middling height; bobbed hair neither long nor short; jaundiced, sickly-looking skin; somewhat prominent cheekbones; her timid, sallow aspect told me all I needed to know. As she came up to the table where I was waiting, I couldn't help but notice her shoes—the plainest black shoes imaginable. And that walk of hers—neither fast nor slow, striding nor mincing.

However, if there wasn't any special attraction, nor did any particular drawbacks present themselves, and there was no reason for the two of us not to get married. The passive personality of this woman in whom I could detect neither freshness nor charm, or anything especially refined, suited me down to the ground. There was no need to affect intellectual leanings in order to win her over, or to worry that she might be comparing me to the preening men who pose in fashion catalogues, and she didn't get worked up if I happened to be late for one of our meetings. The paunch that started appearing in my mid-twenties, my skinny legs and forearms that steadfastly refused to bulk up in spite of my best efforts, the inferiority complex I used to have about the size of my penis—I could rest assured that I wouldn't have to fret about such things on her account.

I've always inclined toward the middle course in life. At school I chose to boss around those who were two or three years my junior, and with whom I could act the ringleader, rather than take my chances with those my own age, and later I chose which college to apply to based on my chances of obtaining a scholarship large enough for my needs. Ultimately, I settled for a job where I would be provided with a decent monthly salary in return for diligently carrying out my allotted tasks, at a company whose small size meant they would value my unremarkable skills. And so it was only natural that I would marry the most run-of-the-mill woman in the world. As for women who were pretty, intelligent, strikingly sensual, the daughters of rich families—they would only have served to disrupt my carefully ordered existence.

In keeping with my expectations, she made for a completely ordinary wife who went about things without any distasteful frivolousness. Every morning she got up at six a.m. to prepare rice and soup, and usually a bit of fish. From adolescence she'd contributed to her family's income through the odd bit of part-time work. She ended up with a job as an assistant instructor at the computer graphics college she'd attended for a year, and was subcontracted by a comics publisher to work on the words for their speech bubbles, which she could do from home.

She was a woman of few words. It was rare for her to demand anything of me, and however late I was in getting home she never took it upon herself to kick up a fuss. Even when our days off happened to coincide, it wouldn't occur to her to suggest we go out somewhere together. While I idled the afternoon away, TV remote in hand, she would shut herself up in her room. More than likely she would spend the time reading, which was practically her only hobby. For some unfathomable reason, reading was something she was able to really immerse herself in—reading books that looked so dull I couldn't even bring myself to so much as take a look inside the covers. Only at mealtimes would she open the door and silently emerge to prepare the food. To be sure, that kind of wife, and that kind of lifestyle, did mean that I was unlikely to find my days particularly stimulating. On the other hand, if I'd had one of those wives whose phones ring on and off all day long with calls from friends or co-workers, or whose nagging periodically leads to screaming rows with their husbands, I would have been grateful when she finally wore herself out.

The only respect in which my wife was at all unusual was that she didn't like wearing a bra. When I was a young man barely out of adolescence, and my wife and I were dating, I happened to put my hand on her back only to find that I couldn't feel a bra strap under her sweater, and when I realized what this meant I became quite aroused. In order to judge whether she might possibly have been trying to tell me something, I spent a minute or two looking at her through new eyes, studying her attitude. The outcome of my studies was that she wasn't, in fact, trying to send any kind of signal. So if not, was it laziness, or just a sheer lack of concern? I couldn't get my head around it. It wasn't as though she had shapely breasts which might suit the "no-bra look." I would have preferred her to go around wearing one that was thickly padded, so that I could save face in front of my acquaintances.

Even in the summer, when I managed to persuade her to wear one for a while, she'd have it unhooked barely a minute after leaving the house. The undone hook would be clearly visible under her thin, light-colored tops, but she wasn't remotely concerned.

I tried reproaching her, lecturing her to layer up with a vest instead of a bra in that sultry heat. She tried to justify herself by saying that she couldn't stand wearing a bra because of the way it squeezed her breasts, and that I'd never worn one myself so I couldn't understand how constricting it felt. Nevertheless, considering I knew for a fact that there were plenty of other women who, unlike her, didn't have anything particularly against bras, I began to have doubts about this hypersensitivity of hers.

In all other respects, the course of our married life ran smoothly. We were approaching the five-year mark, and since we were never madly in love to begin with we were able to avoid falling into that stage of weariness and boredom that can otherwise turn married life into a trial. The only thing was, because we'd decided to put off trying for children until we'd managed to secure a place of our own, which had only happened last autumn, I sometimes wondered whether I would ever get to hear the reassuring sound of a child gurgling "dada," and meaning me. Until a certain day last February, when I came across my wife standing in the kitchen at daybreak in just her nightclothes, I had never considered the possibility that our life together might undergo such an appalling change.

"What are you doing standing there?"

I'd been about to switch on the bathroom light when I was brought up short. It was around four in the morning, and I'd woken up with a raging thirst from the bottle and a half of soju I'd had with dinner, which also meant I was taking longer to come to my senses than usual.

"Hello? I asked what you're doing?"

It was cold enough as it was, but the sight of my wife was even more chilling. Any lingering alcohol-induced drowsiness swiftly passed. She was standing, motionless, in front of the fridge. Her face was submerged in the darkness so I couldn't make out her expression, but the potential options all filled me with fear. Her thick, naturally black hair was fluffed up, disheveled, and she was wearing her usual white ankle-length nightdress.

On such a night, my wife would ordinarily have hurriedly slipped on a cardigan and searched for her shower slippers. How long might she have been standing there like that—barefoot, in thin summer nightwear, ramrod straight as though perfectly oblivious to my repeated interrogation? Her face was turned away from me, and she was standing there so unnaturally still it was almost as if she were some kind of ghost, silently standing its ground.

What was going on? If she couldn't hear me, then perhaps that meant she was sleepwalking.

I went toward her, craning my neck to try to get a look at her face.

"Why are you standing there like that? What's going on?"

When I put my hand on her shoulder I was surprised by her complete lack of reaction. I had no doubt that I was in my right mind and all this was really happening; I had been fully conscious of everything I had done since emerging from the living room, asking her what she was doing, and moving toward her. She was the one standing there completely unresponsive, as though lost in her own world. It was like those rare occasions when, absorbed in a late-night TV drama, she'd failed to notice me arriving home.

But what could there be to absorb her attention in the pale gleam of the fridge's white door, in the pitch-black kitchen at four in the morning?

"Hey!"

Her profile swam toward me out of the darkness. I took in her eyes, bright but not feverish, as her lips slowly parted.

"I had a dream."

Her voice was surprisingly clear.

"A dream? What the hell are you talking about? Do you know what time it is?"

She turned so that her body was facing me, then slowly walked off through the open door into the living room. As she entered the room she stretched out her foot and calmly pushed the door closed. I was left alone in the dark kitchen, looking helplessly on as her retreating figure was swallowed up beyond the door.

I turned on the bathroom light and went in. The cold snap had continued for several days now, consistently hovering around 14°F. I'd showered only a few hours ago, so my plastic shower slippers were still cold and damp. The loneliness of this cruel season began to make itself felt, seeping from the black opening of the ventilation fan above the bath, leaching out of the white tiles covering the floor and walls.

When I went back into the living room my wife was lying down, her legs curled up to her chest, the silence so weighted I might as well have been alone in the room. Of course, this was just my fancy. If I stood perfectly still, held my breath and strained to listen, I was able to hear the faintest sound of breathing coming from where she lay. Yet it didn't sound like the deep, regular breathing of someone who has fallen asleep. I could have reached out to her, and my hand would have encountered her warm skin.

But for some reason I found myself unable to touch her. I didn't even want to reach out to her with words.

For the few moments immediately after I opened my eyes the next morning, when reality had yet to assume its usual concreteness, I lay with the quilt wrapped about me, absentmindedly assessing the quality of the winter sunshine as it filtered into the room through the white curtain. In the middle of this fit of abstraction I happened to glance at the wall clock and jumped up the instant I saw the time, kicked the door open and hurried out of the room. My wife was in front of the fridge.

"Are you crazy? Why didn't you wake me up? What time is . . ."

Something squashed under my foot, stopping me in midsentence. I couldn't believe my eyes.

She was crouching, still wearing her nightclothes, her disheveled, tangled hair a shapeless mass around her face. Around her, the kitchen floor was covered with plastic bags and airtight containers, scattered all over so that there was nowhere I could put my feet without treading on them. Beef for shabu-shabu, belly pork, two sides of black beef shin, some squid in a vacuum-packed bag, sliced eel that my mother-in-law had sent us from the countryside ages ago, dried croaker tied with yellow string, unopened packs of frozen dumplings and endless bundles of unidentified stuff dragged from the depths of the fridge. There was a rustling sound; my wife was busy putting the things around her one by one into black rubbish bags. Eventually I lost control.

"What the hell are you up to now?" I shouted.

She kept on putting the parcels of meat into the rubbish bags, seemingly no more aware of my existence than she had been last night. Beef and pork, pieces of chicken, at least 200,000 won worth of saltwater eel.

"Have you lost your mind? Why on earth are you throwing all this stuff out?"

I hurriedly stumbled my way through the plastic bags and grabbed her wrist, trying to pry the bags from her grip. Stunned to find her fiercely tugging back against me, I almost faltered for a moment, but my outrage soon gave me the strength to overpower her. Massaging her reddened wrist, she spoke in the same ordinary, calm tone of voice she'd used before.

"I had a dream."

Those words again. Her expression as she looked at me was perfectly composed. Just then my mobile rang.

"Damn it!"

I started to fumble through the pockets of my coat, which I'd tossed onto the living room sofa the previous evening. Finally, in the last inside pocket, my fingers closed around my recalcitrant phone.

"I'm sorry. Something's come up, an urgent family matter, so . . . I'm very sorry. I'll be there as quickly as possible. No, I'm going to leave right now. It's just . . . no, I couldn't possibly have you do that. Please wait just a little longer. I'm very sorry. Yes, I really can't talk right now . . ."

I flipped my phone shut and dashed into the bathroom, where I shaved so hurriedly that I cut myself in two places.

"Haven't you even ironed my white shirt?"

There was no answer. I splashed water on myself and rummaged in the laundry basket, searching for yesterday's shirt. Luckily it wasn't too creased. Not once did my wife bother to peer out from the kitchen in the time it took me to get ready, slinging my tie around my neck like a scarf, pulling on my socks, and getting my notebook and wallet together. In the five years we'd been married, this was the first time I'd had to go to work without her handing me my things and seeing me off.

"You're insane! You've completely lost it."

I crammed my feet into my recently purchased shoes, which were too narrow and pinched uncomfortably, threw open the front door and ran out. I checked whether the elevator was going to go all the way up to the top floor, and then dashed down three flights of stairs. Only after I'd managed to jump on the underground train as it was just about to leave did I have time to take in my appearance, reflected in the dark carriage window. I ran my fingers through my hair, did up my tie, and attempted to smooth out the creases in my shirt. My wife's unnaturally serene face, her incongruously firm voice, surfaced in my mind.

I had a dream—she'd said that twice now. Beyond the window, in the dark tunnel, her face flitted by—her face, but unfamiliar, as though I were seeing it for the first time. However, as I had thirty minutes in which to concoct an excuse for my client that would justify my lateness, as well as putting together a draft proposal for today's meeting, there was no time for mulling over the strange behavior of my even-stranger wife. Having said that, I told myself that somehow or other I had to leave the office early today (never mind that in the several months since I'd switched to my new position there hadn't been a single day where I'd got off before midnight), and steeled myself for a confrontation.

Dark woods. No people. The sharp-pointed leaves on the trees, my torn feet. This place, almost remembered, but I'm lost now. Frightened. Cold. Across the frozen ravine, a red barn-like building. Straw matting flapping limp across the door. Roll it up and I'm inside, it's inside. A long bamboo stick strung with great blood-red gashes of meat, blood still dripping down. Try to push past but the meat, there's no end to the meat, and no exit. Blood in my mouth, blood-soaked clothes sucked onto my skin.

Somehow a way out. Running, running through the valley, then suddenly the woods open out. Trees thick with leaves, springtime's green light. Families picnicking, little children running about, and that smell, that delicious smell. Almost painfully vivid. The babbling stream, people spreading out rush mats to sit on, snacking on kimbap. Barbecuing meat, the sounds of singing and happy laughter.

But the fear. My clothes still wet with blood. Hide, hide behind the trees. Crouch down, don't let anybody see. My bloody hands. My bloody mouth. In that barn, what had I done? Pushed that red raw mass into my mouth, felt it squish against my gums, the roof of my mouth, slick with crimson blood.

Chewing on something that felt so real, but couldn't have been, it couldn't. My face, the look in my eyes . . . my face, undoubtedly, but never seen before. Or no, not mine, but so familiar . . . nothing makes sense. Familiar and yet not . . . that vivid, strange, horribly uncanny feeling.

On the dining table my wife had laid out lettuce and soybean paste, plain seaweed soup without the usual beef or clams, and kimchi.

"What the hell? So all because of some ridiculous dream, you've gone and chucked out all the meat? Worth *how* much?"

I got up from my chair and opened the freezer. It was practically empty—nothing but miso powder, chilli powder, frozen fresh chillies, and a pack of minced garlic.

"Just make me some fried eggs. I'm really tired today. I didn't even get to have a proper lunch."

"I threw the eggs out as well."

"*What?*"

"And I've given up milk too."

"This is unbelievable. You're telling me not to eat meat?"

"I couldn't let those things stay in the fridge. It wouldn't be right."

How on earth could she be so self-centered? I stared at her lowered eyes, her expression of cool self-possession. The very idea that there should be this other side to her, one where she selfishly did as she pleased, was astonishing. Who would have thought she could be so unreasonable?

"So you're saying that from now on, there'll be no meat in this house?"

"Well, after all, you usually only eat breakfast at home. And I suppose you often have meat with your lunch and dinner, so . . . it's not as if you'll die if you go without meat just for one meal."

Her reply was so methodical, it was as if she thought that this ridiculous decision of hers was something completely rational and appropriate.

"Oh good, so that's me sorted then. And what about you? You're claiming that you're not going to eat meat at all from now on?" She nodded. "Oh, really? Until when?"

"I suppose . . . forever."

I was lost for words, though at the same time I was aware that choosing a vegetarian diet wasn't quite so rare as it had been in the past. People turn vegetarian for all sorts of reasons: to try and alter their genetic predisposition toward certain allergies, for example, or else because it's seen as more environmentally friendly not to eat meat. Of course, Buddhist priests who have taken certain vows are morally obliged not to participate in the destruction of life, but surely not even impressionable young girls take it quite that far. As far as I was concerned, the only reasonable grounds for altering one's eating habits were the desire to lose weight, an attempt to alleviate certain physical ailments, being possessed by an evil spirit, or having your sleep disturbed by indigestion. In any other case, it was nothing but sheer obstinacy for a wife to go against her husband's wishes as mine had done.

If you'd said that my wife had always been faintly nauseated by meat, then I could have understood it, but in reality it was quite the opposite—ever since we'd got married she had proved herself a more than competent cook, and I'd always been impressed by her way with food. Tongs in one hand and a large pair of scissors in the other, she'd flipped rib meat in a sizzling pan while snipping it into bite-sized pieces, her movements deft and practiced. Her fragrant, caramelized deep-fried belly pork was achieved by marinating the meat in minced ginger and glutinous starch syrup. Her signature dish had been wafer-thin slices of beef seasoned with black pepper and sesame oil, then coated with sticky rice powder as generously as you would with rice cakes or pancakes, and dipped in bubbling shabu-shabu broth. She'd made bibimbap with bean sprouts, minced beef, and pre-soaked rice stir-fried in sesame oil. There had also been a thick chicken and duck soup with large chunks of potato, and a spicy broth packed full of tender clams and mussels, of which I could happily polish off three helpings in a single sitting.

What I was presented with now was a sorry excuse for a meal.

Her chair pulled back at an angle, my wife spooned up some seaweed soup, which was quite clearly going to taste of water and nothing else. She balanced rice and soybean paste on a lettuce leaf, then bundled the wrap into her mouth and chewed it slowly.

I just couldn't understand her. Only then did I realize: I really didn't have a clue when it came to this woman.

"Not eating?" she asked absentmindedly, for all the world like some middle-aged woman addressing her grown-up son. I sat in silence, steadfastly uninterested in this poor excuse for a meal, crunching on kimchi for what felt like an age.

Spring came, and still my wife hadn't backed down. She was as good as her word—I never saw a single piece of meat pass her lips—but I had long since ceased bothering to complain. When a person undergoes such a drastic transformation, there's simply nothing anyone else can do but sit back and let them get on with it.

She grew thinner by the day, so much so that her cheekbones had really become indecently prominent. Without makeup, her complexion resembled that of a hospital patient. If it had all been just another instance of a woman's giving up meat in order to lose weight then there would have been no need to worry, but I was convinced that there was more going on here than a simple case of vegetarianism. No, it had to be that dream she'd mentioned; that was bound to be at the bottom of it all. Although, as a matter of fact, she'd practically stopped sleeping.

No one could describe my wife as especially attentive—often when I returned home late I'd find that she had already fallen asleep. But now I would get in at midnight, and even after I had washed, arranged the bedding, and lain down to sleep, she still wouldn't have come to join me in the living room. She wasn't reading a book, chatting on the Internet, or watching late-night cable TV. The only thing I could think of was that she must have been working on the comics speech bubbles, but there was no way that would have taken up so much time.

She didn't come to bed until around five in the morning, and even then I couldn't say for sure whether she actually spent the next hour asleep or not. Her face haggard and her hair tangled, she would observe me over the breakfast table through red, narrowed eyes. She wouldn't so much as pick up her spoon, never mind actually eat anything.

But what troubled me more was that she now seemed to be actively avoiding sex. In the past, she'd generally been willing to comply with my physical demands, and there'd even been the occasional time when she'd been the one to make the first move. But now, although she didn't make a fuss about it, if my hand so much as brushed her shoulder she would calmly move away. One day I chose to confront her about it.

"What's the problem, exactly?"

"I'm tired."

"Well then, that means you need to eat some meat. That's why you don't have any energy anymore, right? You didn't used to be like this, after all."

"Actually . . ."

"What?"

". . . it's the smell."

"The smell?"

"The meat smell. Your body smells of meat."

This was just too ridiculous for words.

"Didn't you see me just take a shower? So where's this smell coming from, huh?"

"From the same place your sweat comes from," she answered, completely in earnest.

Now and then, all of this struck me as being not so much ridiculous as faintly ominous. What if, by chance, these early-stage symptoms didn't pass? If the hints at hysteria, delusion, weak nerves and so on, that I thought I could detect in what she said, ended up leading to something more?

All the same, I found it difficult to believe that she might genuinely be going soft in the head. Ordinarily she was as taciturn as she'd ever been, and continued to keep the home in good order. On weekends she prepared seasoned vegetable side dishes for us to eat during the week, and even made stir-fried glass noodles with mushrooms instead of the usual meat. It wasn't actually all that strange once you took into account that going vegetarian was apparently in vogue. It was only when she hadn't been able to sleep, when the hollows in her face were even more pronounced than usual, as though she'd deflated from within, and in the morning I would ask what the matter was only to hear "I had a dream." I never inquired as to the nature of this dream. I'd already had to listen once to that crazy spiel about the barn in the dark woods, the face reflected in the pool of blood and all the rest of it, and once had been more than enough.

All because of this agonizing dream, from which I was shut out, had no way of knowing and moreover didn't *want* to know, she continued to waste away. At first she'd slimmed down to the clean, sharp lines of a dancer's physique, and I'd hoped things might stop there, but by now her body resembled nothing so much as the skeletal frame of an invalid. Whenever I found myself troubled by such thoughts, I tried to reassure myself by running through what I knew of her family. Her father worked at a sawmill in a small town, way out in the sticks, where her mother ran a hole-in-the-wall shop, while my sister-in-law and her husband were both regular people, and decent enough—so, at the very least, there didn't seem to be any strain of mental abnormality lurking in my wife's bloodline.

I couldn't think of her family without also recalling the smell of sizzling meat and burning garlic, the sound of shot glasses clinking and the women's noisy conversation emanating from the kitchen. All of them—especially my father-in-law—enjoyed yuk hwe, a kind of beef tartar. I'd seen my mother-in-law gut a live fish, and my wife and her sister were both perfectly competent when it came to hacking a chicken into pieces with a butcher's cleaver. I'd always liked my wife's earthy vitality, the way she would catch cockroaches by smacking them with the palm of her hand. She really had been the most ordinary woman in the world.

Even given the extreme unpredictability of her condition, I wasn't prepared to consider taking her for an urgent medical consultation, much less a course of treatment. There's nothing wrong with her, I told myself, this kind of thing isn't even a real illness. I resisted the temptation to indulge in introspection. This strange situation had nothing to do with me.

The morning before I had the dream, I was mincing frozen meat—remember? You got angry.

"Damn it, what the hell are you doing squirming like that? You've never been squeamish before."

If you knew how hard I've always worked to keep my nerves in check. Other people just get a bit flustered, but for me everything gets confused, speeds up. Quick, quicker. The hand holding the knife was working so quickly, I felt heat prickle the back of my neck. My hand, the chopping board, the meat, and then the knife, slicing cold into my finger.

A drop of red blood already blossoming out of the cut. Rounder than round. Sticking the finger in my mouth calmed me. The scarlet color, and now the taste, sweetness masking something else, left me strangely pacified.

Later that day, when you sat down to a meal of bulgogi, you spat out the second mouthful and picked out something glittering.

"What the hell is this?" you yelled. "A chip off the knife?"

I gazed vacantly at your distorted face as you raged.

"Just think what would have happened if I'd swallowed it! I was this close to dying!"

Why didn't this agitate me like it should have done? Instead, I became even calmer. A cool hand on my forehead. Suddenly, everything around me began to slide away, as though pulled back on an ebbing tide. The dining table, you, all the kitchen furniture. I was alone, the only thing remaining in all of infinite space.

Dawn of the next day. The pool of blood in the barn . . . I first saw the face reflected there.

"What's wrong with your lips? Haven't you done your makeup?"

I took my shoes off again and dragged my flustered wife, who'd already put on her coat, into the front room.

"Were you really going to go out looking like this?" The two of us were reflected in the dressing table mirror. "Do your makeup again."

She gently shrugged off my hand, opened her compact and

patted the powder puff over her face. The powder made her face somewhat blurry, covering it in motes. The rich coral lipstick she always used to wear, and without which her lips were ashen, went some way to alleviating her sickly pallor. I was reassured.

"We're late. Come on, hurry up."

I opened the front door and hurried her out, staring impatiently as she fumbled with her dark blue sneakers. They didn't go with her black trench coat, but it couldn't be helped. She had no smart shoes left, having thrown out anything made from leather.

As soon as the car engine started I switched on the radio to listen to the traffic bulletin, paying particular attention to any mention of issues near the Korean-Chinese restaurant that the boss had reserved. Once I'd made sure it wouldn't be quicker to go by another route, I fastened my seat belt and released the handbrake. My wife spent a minute fussing with her coat, and finally managed to fasten her seat belt after a couple of failed attempts.

"I need this evening to go well. You know it's the first time the boss has invited me to one of these dinners."

We only just managed to get to the restaurant in time, and even then only because I'd gone flat out on the main road. The two-story building, fronted by a spacious car park, was clearly a sophisticated establishment.

The cold of late winter was stubbornly lingering, and my wife looked chilly as she stood in the car park dressed in only a thin spring coat. She hadn't said a single word on the way here, but I convinced myself that this wouldn't be a problem. There's nothing wrong with keeping quiet; after all, hadn't women traditionally been expected to be demure and restrained?

My boss, the managing director and the executive director had already arrived, along with their wives. The section chief and his wife turned up a few minutes after us, completing the party. There were nods and smiles all around as we exchanged greetings, took off our coats and hung them up. My boss's wife, an imposing woman with finely plucked eyebrows and a large jade necklace clacking at her throat, escorted my wife and me over to the dining table, already laid for what promised to be a lavish meal, and sat down at the head of the table. The others all seemed quite at ease, like regulars. I took my seat, careful not to be seen to gawp at the ornate ceiling, which was as elaborately decorated as the eaves of a traditional building. My gaze was arrested by the sight of goldfish swimming lazily in a glass bowl, and I turned to address my wife, but what I saw there brought me up short.

She was wearing a slightly clinging black blouse, and to my utter mortification I saw that the outline of her nipples was clearly visible through the fabric. Without a doubt, she'd come out without a bra. When the other guests surreptitiously craned their necks, no doubt wanting to be sure that they really were seeing what they thought they were, the eyes of the executive director's wife met mine. Feigning composure, I registered the curiosity, astonishment, and contempt that were revealed in turn in her eyes.

I could feel my cheeks flushing. All too conscious of my wife, sitting there hollow-eyed and making no attempt to join in with the other women's exchange of pleasantries, I controlled myself and decided that the best thing to do, the only thing to do, was to act natural and pretend that there was nothing untoward.

"Did you have any problems finding the place?" my boss's wife asked me.

"No, no, I've been past here once or twice before. In fact, I'd been thinking of coming here myself."

"Ah, I see . . . yes, the garden has turned out quite well, hasn't it? You ought to try coming in the daytime; you can see the flower beds through that window over there."

But by the time the food began to be served, the strain of maintaining a casual facade, which I had just about managed so far, was bringing me close to breaking point.

The first thing placed in front of us was an exquisite dish of mung-bean jelly, dressed with thin slivers of green-pea jelly, mushrooms and beef. Up until then my wife had merely sat and observed the scene in silence, but just as the waiter was on the point of ladling some onto her plate, she finally opened her mouth.

"I won't eat it."

She'd spoken very quietly, but the other guests all instantly stopped what they were doing, directing glances of surprise and wonder at her emaciated body.

"I don't eat meat," she said, slightly louder this time.

"My word, so you're one of those 'vegetarians,' are you?" my boss asked. "Well, I knew that some people in other countries are strict vegetarians, of course. And even here, you know, it does seem that attitudes are beginning to change a little. Now and then there'll be someone claiming that eating meat is bad . . . after all, I suppose giving up meat in order to live a long life isn't all that unreasonable, is it?"

"But surely it isn't possible to live without eating meat?" his wife asked with a smile.

The waiter whisked nine plates away, leaving my wife's still-gleaming plate on the table. The conversation naturally continued on the topic of vegetarianism.

"Do you remember those mummified human remains they discovered recently? Five hundred thousand years old, apparently, and even back then humans were hunting for meat—they could tell that from the skeletons. Meat eating is a fundamental human instinct, which means vegetarianism goes against human nature, right? It just isn't natural."

"People mainly used to turn vegetarian because they subscribed to a certain ideology . . . I've been to various doctors myself, to have some tests done and see if there was anything in particular I ought to be avoiding, but everywhere I went I was told something different . . . in any case, the idea of a special diet always made me feel uncomfortable. It seems to me that one shouldn't be too narrow-minded when it comes to food."

"People who arbitrarily cut out this or that food, even though they're not actually allergic to anything—that's what I would call narrow-minded," the executive director's wife chimed in; she had been sneaking sideways glances at my wife's breasts for some time now. "A balanced diet goes hand in hand with a balanced mind, don't you think?" And now she loosed her arrow directly at my wife. "Was there some special reason for your becoming a vegetarian? Health reasons, for example . . . or religious, perhaps?"

"No." Her cool reply proved that she was completely oblivious to how delicate the situation had become. All of a sudden, a shiver ran through me—because I had a gut feeling that I knew what she was about to say next.

"I had a dream."

I hurriedly spoke over her.

"For a long time my wife used to suffer from gastroenteritis, which was so acute that it disturbed her sleep, you see. A dietitian advised her to give up meat, and her symptoms got a lot better after that."

Only then did the others nod in understanding.

"Well, I must say, I'm glad I've still never sat down with a proper vegetarian. I'd hate to share a meal with someone who considers eating meat repulsive, just because that's how they themselves personally feel . . . don't you agree?"

"Imagine you were snatching up a wriggling baby octopus with your chopsticks and chomping it to death—and the woman across from you glared like you were some kind of animal. That must be how it feels to sit down and eat with a vegetarian!"

The group broke out into laughter, and I was conscious of each and every separate laugh. Needless to say, my wife didn't so much as crack a smile. By now, everyone was busy making sure that their mouths were fully occupied with eating, so that it wouldn't be up to them to try and fill the awkward silences that were now peppering the conversation. It was clear that they were all uncomfortable.

The next dish was fried chicken in a chili and garlic sauce, and after that was raw tuna. My wife sat there immobile while everyone else tucked in, her nipples resembling a pair of acorns as they pushed against the fabric of her blouse. Her gaze roamed intently over the rapidly working mouths of the other guests, delving into every nook and cranny as though intending to soak up every little detail.

By the time the twelve magnificent courses were over, my wife had eaten nothing but salad and kimchi, and a little bit of squash porridge. She hadn't even touched the sticky-rice porridge, as they had used a special recipe involving beef stock to give it a rich, luxurious taste. Gradually, the other guests learned to ignore her presence and the conversation started to flow again. Now and then, perhaps out of pity, they made an effort to include me, but in my heart of hearts I knew that they wanted to keep a certain distance between us.

When fruit was brought out for dessert my wife ate one small slice of apple and a single orange segment.

"You're not hungry? But, my goodness, you've barely eaten anything!" There was something flamboyant about the friendly, sociable tone in which my boss's wife expressed her concern. But the demure, apologetic smile that was the only reasonable response never came, and without even having the grace to look embarrassed, my wife simply stared baldly at my boss's wife. That stare appalled everyone present. Did she not even recognize the situation for what it was? Was it possible that she hadn't grasped the status of the elegant middle-aged woman facing her? What shadowy recesses lurked in her mind, what secrets I'd never suspected? In that moment, she was utterly unknowable.

I didn't know what I could do, exactly, but I knew that I had to do something.

That was the dilemma which tormented me as I drove home. My wife, on the other hand, appeared entirely unperturbed, seemingly unaware of how disgraceful her behavior had been. She just sat there resting her head against the sloping car window, apparently on the point of dozing off. Naturally, I got angry. Did she want to see her husband get fired? What the hell did she think she was doing?

But I had a feeling that none of it would make the slightest bit of difference. Neither rage nor persuasion would succeed in moving her, and I would be unable to take matters into my own hands.

After washing and putting on her nightclothes she disappeared into her own room rather than getting ready to sleep in the living room as we usually did. I was left pacing up and down when I heard the phone ring: my mother-in-law.

"How is everything with you? I hadn't heard a thing for such a long time . . ."

"I'm sorry about that. It's just that I've been so busy lately . . . is my father-in-law in good health?"

"Oh, nothing ever changes with us. Are things going well at work?"

I hesitated. "I'm fine. But as for my wife . . ."

"What about Yeong-hye, what's the matter?" Her voice was laced with worry. She had never seemed to show much of an interest in her second daughter, but I suppose one's children are one's children, after all.

"The thing is, she's stopped eating meat."

"What did you say?"

"She's stopped eating any kind of meat at all, even fish—all she lives on is vegetables. It's been several months now."

"What kind of talk is this? Surely you can always just tell her not to follow this diet."

"Oh, I've told her, all right, but she still goes ahead and defies me. And what's more, she's even imposed this ridiculous diet on me—I can't remember the last time I tasted meat in this house."

My mother-in-law was lost for words, and I used her speechlessness as an opportunity to turn the screw a little tighter. "She's become very weak. I'm not sure exactly how serious it is . . ."

"I can't have this. Is Yeong-hye there? Pass her the phone."

"She's gone to bed now. I'll tell her to call tomorrow morning."

"No, leave it. I'll call. How can that child be so defiant? Oh, you must be ashamed of her!"

After hanging up I riffled through my notebook and dialed my sister-in-law In-hye's number.

My ears were assaulted by the sound of her young son bellowing "hello?" down the line.

"Please put your mother on."

In-hye, who quickly took the receiver from her son, resembled my wife quite closely, but her eyes were larger and prettier, and overall she was much more feminine.

"Hello?"

Her voice as it sounded over the phone, always somehow more distinct than in person, never failed to send me into a state of sexual arousal. I informed her of my wife's newfound vegetarianism in the same way as I had just done with her mother, listened to exactly the same sequence of astonishment followed by an apology, and put down the phone after accepting her assurances. I considered repeating the process by calling my wife's younger brother, Yeong-ho, but decided that that would be overdoing it.

Dreams of murder.

Murderer or murdered. . . . hazy distinctions, boundaries wearing thin. Familiarity bleeds into strangeness, certainty becomes impossible. Only the violence is vivid enough to stick. A sound, the elasticity of the instant when the metal struck the victim's head . . . the shadow that crumpled and fell gleams cold in the darkness.

They come to me now more times than I can count. Dreams overlaid with dreams, a palimpsest of horror. Violent acts perpetrated by night. A hazy feeling I can't pin down . . . but remembered as blood-chillingly definite.

Intolerable loathing, so long suppressed. Loathing I've always tried to mask with affection. But now the mask is coming off.

That shuddering, sordid, gruesome, brutal feeling. Nothing else remains. Murderer or murdered, experience too vivid to not be real. Determined, disillusioned. Lukewarm, like slightly cooled blood.

Everything starts to feel unfamiliar. As if I've come up to the back of something. Shut up behind a door without a handle. Perhaps I'm only now coming face-to-face with the thing that has always been here. It's dark. Everything is being snuffed out in the pitch-black darkness.

Contrary to what I'd hoped, my mother- and sister-in-law's efforts at persuasion had not the slightest influence on my wife's eating habits. At the weekend, the phone rang and my wife picked up.

"Yeong-hye," my father-in-law bellowed, "are you still not eating meat?" He'd never used a telephone in his life, and I could hear his excited shouts emerging from the receiver. "What d'you think you're playing at, hey? Acting like this at your age, what on earth must Mr. Cheong think?" My wife stood there in perfect silence, holding the receiver to her ear. "Why don't you answer? Can you hear me?"

A pan of soup was boiling on the stove, so my wife put the receiver down on the table without a word and disappeared into the kitchen. I stood there for a few moments listening to my father-in-law raging impotently, unaware that there was no one on the other end, then took pity on him and picked up the receiver.

"I'm sorry, Father-in-law."

"No, I'm the one who's ashamed."

It shocked me to hear this patriarchal man apologize—in the five years I'd known him, I'd never once heard such words pass his lips. Shame and empathy just didn't suit him. He never tired of boasting about having received the Order of Military Merit for serving in Vietnam, and not only was his voice extremely loud, it was the voice of a man with strongly fixed ideas. *I myself, in Vietnam . . . seven Vietcong . . .* as his son-in-law, I was only too familiar with the beginning of his monologue. According to my wife, he had whipped her over the calves until she was eighteen years old.

"In any case, you're coming up next month so let's sit her down and have it out then."

The family get-together scheduled for the second Sunday this coming June was clearly going to be a very big deal. Even if no one said it openly, it was plain to see that they were all getting ready to give my wife a dressing-down.

Whether or not my wife was actually aware of any of this, she never seemed in the least bit perturbed. Aside from the fact that she deliberately continued to avoid sleeping with me—she'd even taken to sleeping in trousers—on the surface we were still a regular married couple. The only thing that had changed was that in the early hours of the morning, when I groped for my alarm clock, turned it off and sat up, she would be lying there ramrod straight, her eyes gazing upward in the darkness. After the meal at the restaurant, other people in the company had been noticeably cool toward me, but once the project I'd pushed through began to yield some far-from-negligible profits, all that unpleasantness appeared to have been entirely forgotten.

I sometimes told myself that even though the woman I was living with was a little odd, nothing particularly bad would come of it. I thought I could get by perfectly well just thinking of her as a stranger, or no, as a sister, or even a maid, someone who puts food on the table and keeps the house in good order. But it was no easy thing for a man in the prime of his life, for whom married life had always gone entirely without a hitch, to have his physical needs go unsatisfied for such a long period of time. So yes, one night when I returned home late and somewhat inebriated after a meal with colleagues, I grabbed hold of my wife and pushed her to the floor. Pinning down her struggling arms and tugging off her trousers, I became unexpectedly aroused. She put up a surprisingly strong resistance and, spitting out vulgar curses all the while, it took me three attempts before I managed to insert myself successfully. Once that had happened, she lay there in the dark staring up at the ceiling, her face blank, as though she were a "comfort woman" dragged in against her will, and I was the Japanese soldier demanding her services. As soon as I finished, she rolled over and buried her face in the quilt. I went to have a shower, and by the time I returned to bed she was lying there with her eyes closed as if nothing had happened, or as though everything had somehow sorted itself out during the time I'd spent washing myself.

After this first time, it was easier for me to do it again, but each time, I would be seized by strange, ominous premonitions. I was thick-skinned by nature, and certainly wasn't in the habit of entertaining outlandish notions, but the darkness and silence of the living room would strike a chill through me all the same. The following morning, sitting with my wife at the breakfast table— her lips pressed firmly closed as per usual, clearly not paying the slightest bit of attention to anything I might be saying—I would be unable to conceal a feeling of abhorrence when I looked across at her. I couldn't stand the way her expression, which made it seem as though she were a woman of bitter experience, who had suffered many hardships, niggled at my conscience.

It was the evening three days before the family gathering. That day, the humidity in Seoul was the highest on record and the air-conditioning was blasting out in all the big shops. After spending all day in the office I was starting to shiver, and so I returned home a little earlier than usual. On opening the front door and catching sight of my wife, I stepped hastily inside and closed the door behind me; it was a corridor apartment, and the last thing I needed was for someone to pass by and peek in. She was sitting leaning against the decorative television cabinet, peeling potatoes, wearing thin white cotton trousers but with her upper body bare to the waist. She had now lost so much weight that her breasts were little more than a pair of small bumps beneath her sharply protruding collarbones.

"Why have you taken your clothes off?" I asked her, trying to force out a laugh.

"Because it's hot," she answered, neither raising her head nor pausing in what she was doing.

I gritted my teeth. Look at me, I willed her, but without saying the words out loud. Look at me and laugh. Show me that your answer was just a joke. But she didn't laugh. It was eight in the evening and the door to the balcony was open, which meant that the apartment was quite cool, and my wife's shoulders were covered in goose pimples like tiny sesame seeds. The potato peelings were piled up in heaps on sheets of newspaper. Thirty-odd remaining potatoes formed a small mound.

"What are you planning to do with them?" I asked, affecting perfect composure.

"Steam them."

"All of them?"

"Mm-hm."

I laughed falteringly and waited for her to laugh in response. But she didn't laugh. She didn't even lift her head.

"I was just, you know . . . hungry."

Dreams of my hands around someone's throat, throttling them, grabbing the swinging ends of their long hair and hacking it all off, sticking my finger into their slippery eyeball. Those drawn-out waking hours, a pigeon's dull colors in the street and my resolve falters, my fingers flexing to kill. Next door's cat, its bright tormenting eyes, my fingers that could squeeze that brightness out. My trembling legs, the cold sweat on my brow. I become a different person, a different person rises up inside me, devours me, those hours . . .

Saliva pooling in my mouth. The butcher's shop, and I have to clamp my hand over my mouth. Along the length of my tongue to my lips, slick with saliva. Leaking out between my lips, trickling down.

If only I could sleep. If I could shrug off consciousness for even just an hour. The house is cold on all these nights, more nights than I can count, when I wake up and pace about in bare feet. Chill like rice or soup that has been left to go cold. Nothing is visible outside the black window. The dark front door rattles now and then, but no one comes to knock on the door or anything like that. By the time I come back to bed and put my hand under the quilt, all the warmth is gone.

Sleeping in five-minute snatches. Slipping out of fuzzy consciousness, it's back—the dream. Can't even call it that now. Animal eyes gleaming wild, presence of blood, unearthed skull, again those eyes. Rising up from the pit of my stomach. Shuddering awake, my hands, need to see my hands. Breathe. My fingernails still soft, my teeth still gentle.

Can only trust my breasts now. I like my breasts, nothing can be killed by them. Hand, foot, tongue, gaze, all weapons from which nothing is safe. But not my breasts. With my round breasts, I'm okay. Still okay. So why do they keep on shrinking? Not even round anymore. Why? Why am I changing like this? Why are my edges all sharpening—what I am going to gouge?

The sunny south-facing apartment was on the seventeenth floor. True, the view out east was obscured by other buildings, but to the rear the mountains were visible in the distance.

"Now you've forgotten all your worries," my father-in-law pronounced, taking up his spoon and chopsticks. "Completely seized the moment!"

Even before she got married, my sister-in-law In-hye had managed to secure an apartment with the income she received from managing a cosmetics store. Leading up to her pregnancy, the store had expanded to three times its original size, and after the birth she insisted on stopping by—only at night, and just for a short while—to make sure that everything was running smoothly in her absence. As soon as my nephew Ji-woo turned three and went to a nursery, she'd apparently started spending all day in the shop again.

I envied her husband. He was an art college graduate who liked to pose as an artist, yet didn't contribute a single penny to their household finances. True, he had some property that he'd inherited, but he didn't bring in a salary—in fact, his activities were limited to sitting around and not doing an awful lot of anything. Now that In-hye had rolled up her sleeves and gone back to work, her husband was free to spend his whole life messing about with "art," without a single worry to trouble his comfortable existence. Not only that, but In-hye was also a skilled cook, just as my wife used to be. Seeing the lunch table she had swiftly set made me feel a sudden pang of hunger. Taking in her nicely filled-out figure, big, double-lidded eyes, and demure manner of speaking, I sorely regretted the many things it seemed I'd ended up losing somehow or other, to have left me in my current plight.

Neither complimenting the house nor thanking her sister for taking the trouble to prepare the food, my wife sat quietly eating rice and kimchi. Those were the only things she touched. Mayonnaise contained egg, so that was another thing off the menu for her—she didn't so much as stick her chopsticks into the mouthwatering salad.

Her face was blanched, a result of protracted insomnia. A stranger coming across her in the street would have assumed she was a hospital patient. A little earlier, pretty much as soon as we'd both come in through the front door, she'd been summoned to the master bedroom; after a while, my sister-in-law was the first to emerge, and judging from her baffled expression I guessed that my wife had come out without a bra. Sure enough, when I looked closely I could see her light-brown nipples showing through like smudges on the cotton.

"How much was the deposit here?"

"Really? We went to look at the real estate site yesterday; this apartment had already gone up to around fifty million won. Because next year they will have completed the underground line extension, you see."

"My brother-in-law certainly has a good head for this kind of thing."

"What did I do? It was all down to my wife."

While our polite, amiable conversation carried on in intermittent bursts, the children seemed unable to sit still, hitting each other and making an almighty racket, pausing only to stuff their mouths with food.

"Sister-in-law," I asked, "did you prepare all this food yourself?"

She gave me a half smile.

"Well, I've been doing it bit by bit since the day before yesterday. And those, the seasoned oysters, I went to the market expressly to get because I know Yeong-hye likes them . . . and she hasn't even touched them."

I held my breath. Here it comes, I thought.

"Enough!" my father-in-law yelled. "You, Yeong-hye! After all I told you, your own father!"

This outburst was followed by In-hye's roundly rebuking my wife. "Do you truly intend to go on like this? Human beings need certain nutrients . . . if you intend to follow a vegetarian diet you should sit down and draw up a proper, well-balanced meal plan. Just look at your face!"

So far my wife's brother Yeong-ho was keeping his own counsel, so his wife decided to have her say instead. "When I saw her I thought she was a different person. I'd heard about it from my husband, but I never would have guessed that going vegetarian could damage your body like that."

My mother-in-law brought in dishes of stir-fried beef, sweet and sour pork, steamed chicken, and octopus noodles, arranging them on the table in front of my wife.

"This whole vegetarian business stops right now," she said.

"This one, and this, and this—hurry up and eat them. How could you have got into this wretched state when there's not a thing in the world you can't eat?"

"Well, what are you waiting for? Come on, eat up," my father-in-law boomed.

"You must eat, Yeong-hye," In-hye admonished. "You'll have more energy if you do. Everyone needs a certain amount of energy while they're alive. Even priests who enter the temple don't take their austerities too far—they might be celibate, but they're still able to live active lives."

The children were staring wide-eyed at my wife. She turned her blank gaze on her family, as if she couldn't fathom the reason for all this sudden fuss.

A strained silence ensued. I surveyed in turn my father-in-law's swarthy cheeks; my mother-in-law's face, so full of wrinkles I couldn't believe it had once been that of a young woman, her eyes filled with worry; In-hye's anxiously raised eyebrows; her husband's affected attitude of being no more than a casual bystander; the passive but seemingly displeased expressions of Yeong-ho and his wife. I expected my wife to say something in her own defense, but the sole, silent answer she made to all those glaring faces was to set the pair of chopsticks she had picked up back down on the table.

A small flurry of unease ran through the assembled family. This time, my mother-in-law picked up some sweet and sour pork with her chopsticks and thrust it right up in front of my wife's mouth, saying, "Here. Come on, hurry up and eat." Mouth closed, my wife stared at her mother as though entirely ignorant of the rules of etiquette. "Open your mouth right now. You don't like it?

Well, try this instead, then." She tried the same thing with stir-fried beef, and when my wife kept her mouth shut just as before, set the beef down and picked up some dressed oysters. "Haven't you liked these since you were little? You used to want to eat them all the time—"

"Yes, I remember that too," In-hye chimed in, backing up her mother by making it seem as though my wife's not eating oysters were the ultimate big deal. "I always think of you when I see oysters, Yeong-hye."

As the chopsticks holding the dressed oysters gradually neared my wife's averted mouth, she twisted away violently.

"Eat it quickly! My arm hurts . . ."

My mother-in-law's arm was actually trembling. Eventually, my wife stood up.

"I won't eat it."

For the first time in a long while, her speech was clear and distinct.

"*What?*" my wife's father and brother, who were both similarly hot tempered, yelled in concert. Yeong-ho's wife quickly grabbed her husband's arm.

"My heart will pack in if this goes on any longer!" my father-in-law shouted at Yeong-hye. "Don't you understand what your father's telling you? If he tells you to eat, you eat!"

I expected an answer from my wife along the lines of "I'm sorry, Father, but I just can't eat it," but all she said was "I do not eat meat"—clearly enunciated, and seemingly not the least bit apologetic.

My mother-in-law gathered up the chopsticks with an attitude of despair. Her old woman's face seemed on the brink of crumpling into tears, tears that would explode from her eyes and then course down her wrinkled cheeks in silence. My father-in-law took up a pair of chopsticks. He used them to pick up a piece of sweet and sour pork and stood tall in front of my wife, who turned away.

My father-in-law stooped slightly as he thrust the pork at my wife's face, a lifetime's rigid discipline unable to disguise his advanced age.

"Eat it! Listen to what your father's telling you and eat. Everything I say is for your own good. So why act like this if it makes you ill?"

The fatherly affection that was almost choking the old man made a powerful impression on me, and I was moved to tears in spite of myself. Probably everyone gathered there felt the same. With one hand my wife pushed away his chopsticks, which were shaking silently in empty space.

"Father, I don't eat meat."

In an instant, his flat palm cleaved the empty space. My wife cupped her cheek in her hand.

"Father!" In-hye cried out, grabbing his arm. His lips twitched as though his agitation had not yet passed off. I'd known of his incredibly violent temperament for some time, but it was the first time I'd directly witnessed him striking someone.

"Mr. Cheong, Yeong-ho, the two of you come here."

I approached my wife hesitantly. He'd hit her so hard that the blood showed through the skin of her cheek. Her breathing was ragged, and it seemed that her composure had finally been shattered. "Take hold of Yeong-hye's arms, both of you."

"What?"

"If she eats it once, she'll eat it again. It's preposterous, everyone eats meat!"

Yeong-ho stood up, looking as though he were finding this whole episode distasteful.

"Sister, would you please just eat? Or after all, it would be simple enough just to pretend. Do you have to make such a thing about it in front of Father?"

"What kind of talk is that?" my father-in-law yelled. "Grab her arms, quickly. You too, Mr. Cheong."

"Father, why are you doing this?" In-hye took hold of her father's right arm.

Having thrown down the chopsticks, he now picked up a piece of pork with his fingers and approached my wife. She was hesitantly backing away when her brother seized her and sat her down.

"Sister, just behave, okay? Just eat what he gives you."

"Father, I beg you, stop this," In-hye entreated him, but he shook her off and thrust the pork at my wife's lips. A moaning sound came from her tightly closed mouth. She was unable to say even a single word in case, when she opened her mouth to speak, the meat found its way in.

"Father!" Yeong-ho shouted, apparently wanting to dissuade him, though he himself didn't release his grip on my wife.

"Mm-mm. . . . mm!"

My father-in-law mashed the pork to a pulp on my wife's lips as she struggled in agony. Though he parted her lips with his strong fingers, he could do nothing about her clenched teeth.

Eventually he flew into a passion again, and struck her in the face once more.

"Father!"

Though In-hye sprang at him and held him by the waist, in the instant that the force of the slap had knocked my wife's mouth open he'd managed to jam the pork in. As soon as the strength in Yeong-ho's arms was visibly exhausted, my wife growled and spat out the meat. An animal cry of distress burst from her lips.

"Get away!"

At first, she drew up her shoulders and seemed about to flee in the direction of the front door, but then she turned back and picked up the fruit knife that had been lying on the dining table.

"Yeong-hye?" My mother-in-law's voice, which seemed about to break, drew a trembling line through the brutal silence. The children burst into noisy sobbing, unable to suppress it any longer.

Jaw clenched, her intent stare facing each one of us down in turn, my wife brandished the knife.

"Stop her . . ."

"Stay back!"

Blood ribboned out of her wrist. The shock of red splashed over white china. As her knees buckled and she crumpled to the floor, the knife was wrested from her by In-hye's husband, who until then had sat through the whole thing as an idle spectator.

"What are you doing? Somebody fetch a towel, at least!" Every inch the special forces graduate, he stopped the bleeding with practiced skill, and picked my wife up in his arms. "Quickly, go down and start the engine!"

I groped for my shoes. The ones I'd picked up weren't a pair, so I had to swap them before I was able to open the front door and go out.

. . . the dog that sank its teeth into my leg is chained up to Father's motorcycle. With its singed tail bandaged to my calf wound, a traditional remedy

Mother insisted on, I go out and stand at the main gate. I am nine years old, and the summer heat is stifling. The sun has gone down, and still the sweat is running off me. The dog, too, is panting, its red tongue lolling. A white, handsome-looking dog, bigger even than me. Up until it bit the big man's daughter, everyone in the village always thought it could do no wrong.

While Father ties the dog to the tree and scorches it with a lamp, he says it isn't to be flogged. He says he heard somewhere that driving a dog to keep running until the point of death is considered a milder punishment. The motorcycle engine starts, and Father begins to drive in a circle. The dog runs along behind. Two laps, three laps, they circle around. Without moving a muscle I stand just inside the gate watching Whitey, eyes rolling and gasping for breath, gradually exhaust himself. Every time his gleaming eyes meet my own I glare even more fiercely.

Bad dog, you'd bite me?

Once it has gone five laps, the dog is frothing at the mouth. Blood drips from its throat, which is being choked with the rope. Constantly groaning through its damaged throat, the dog is dragged along the ground. At six laps, the dog vomits blackish-red blood, trickling from its mouth and open throat. As blood and froth mix together, I stand stiffly upright and stare at those two glittering eyes. Seven laps, and while waiting for the dog to come into view, Father looks behind and sees that it is in fact dangling limply from the motorcycle. I look at the dog's four juddering legs, its raised eyelids, the blood and water in its dead eyes.

That evening there was a feast at our house. All the middle-aged men from the market alleyways came, everyone my father considered worth knowing. The saying goes that for a wound caused by a dog bite to heal you have to eat that same dog, and I did scoop up a mouthful for myself. No, in fact I ate an entire bowlful with rice. The smell of burnt flesh, which the perilla seeds couldn't wholly mask, pricked my nose. I remember the two eyes that had watched me, while the dog was made to run on, while he vomited blood mixed with froth, and how later they had seemed to appear, flickering, on the surface of the soup. But I don't care. I really didn't care.

The women stayed behind in the house in order to calm the children down, Yeong-ho saw to my mother-in-law, who had fainted, and my brother-in-law and I took my wife to the casualty department of a nearby hospital. Now no longer in a critical condition, she was transferred to a general two-patient room, and only then did we two men become aware that our clothes were stained with dried blood.

My wife fell asleep with an IV needle inserted into her right arm. The two of us observed her sleeping face in silence. As though some sort of solution were inscribed there. As though, if I only kept on examining her face, I would be able to figure out the answer.

"Could you step outside for a moment?" I asked my brother-in-law. His expression suggested that he had something he wanted to get off his chest, but he limited himself to a noncommittal "all right." I pulled out won from my pocket, which was all I could find in there, and handed it over.

"Please use this to buy a set of clothes from the store."

"Me? Ah, my wife will bring me some clean clothes when she comes around later."

Yeong-ho and his wife showed up that evening, with In-hye. Apparently my father-in-law still hadn't calmed down. Their mother kept stubbornly insisting on coming to the hospital, but Yeong-ho was adamant that she wasn't to go anywhere near the place.

"What on earth went on back there?" Yeong-ho's wife exclaimed. "And right in front of the children . . ." She must have been crying, as her makeup had run and her eyes were swollen. "Your father went too far, you know. How can he hit his daughter in front of her husband? Has he always been like this?"

"Of course, he's always been quick-tempered," In-hye admitted. "Haven't you seen how Yeong-ho takes after him? But still, now he's older it's not so bad . . ."

Yeong-ho looked put out. "Why are you putting the blame on me?"

"Though after all," In-hye continued, ignoring him, "Yeong-hye refused to say a single word to him, so he was bound to get upset, you know—I mean, she is his daughter . . ."

"Force-feeding her meat was certainly taking it too far, but what made her decide to stop eating it in the first place? And then why the knife? I've never seen such a thing in all my life. However will she look her husband in the face?" Yeong-ho's wife looked still half in shock.

While In-hye was examining my wife, I changed into her husband's T-shirt and went to the sauna upstairs. I washed off the black congealed blood under the shower's lukewarm stream of water. I looked at myself in the mirror, frowning. The whole affair made my flesh crawl. It just didn't seem real. Right then, thinking about my wife didn't cause me shock or confusion so much as an intense feeling of disgust.

After In-hye had gone home, the only people left in the general ward aside from my wife and me were a schoolgirl who'd been admitted with a ruptured intestine, and her parents. They kept on darting sideways glances at me while I stood watch at my wife's bedside, and I could see perfectly well that they were whispering together. But any minute now this long Sunday would be over and Monday would begin, which meant I would no longer have to look at this woman. I expected that Yeong-ho would take my place, and that the day after tomorrow my wife would be discharged. Discharged—in other words, I would once again have to live with this strange, frightening woman, the two of us in the same house. It was a prospect I found difficult to contemplate.

At nine o'clock the next evening I visited the ward. Yeong-ho greeted me with a smile.

"You must be tired, no?" he said.

"How are the children?"

"Ji-woo's dad's staying with them today."

If only my colleagues had decided to go for drinks after work, I would have had the perfect excuse to avoid the ward for another two hours. But it was Monday, so there was no chance of any such reprieve.

"How's my wife been?"

"She's just been sleeping. You can see that without having to ask. She ate what they gave her . . . it seems she's going to be okay."

Yeong-ho was clearly trying to be considerate, and he did manage to soothe my sharp mood a little. A short while after he left, and just as I was thinking to myself that I ought to loosen my tie and freshen up, someone knocked on the door of the ward.

To my surprise, it was my mother-in-law.

"I'm so ashamed to face you," she began babbling as soon as she came near me.

"There's no need for that. How are you?"

She took a deep breath.

"Well, you see how it is with old age, the slightest shock . . ."

She'd brought a shopping bag with her, which she now thrust at me.

"What's this?"

"Something I prepared before we came up to Seoul. You waste away after months without meat, it seems, so . . . eat this together, the two of you. It's black goat. I was afraid that if In-hye and her husband found out they might try and stop me from coming. Try feeding it to Yeong-hye, just tell her it's herbal medicine. I put a load of medicinal stuff in to mask the smell. She's become such a scrawny thing, just a ghost, and now what with losing all that blood . . ."

I was beginning to get sick and tired of this stubborn "maternal affection."

"There's no stovetop here, is there? I'll go and see if they have one in the nurses' room." She took one of the packets out of her bag and left. Repeatedly winding my tie around my hand and clenching it into a ball, I felt myself get more and more worked up, as the irritation returned that Yeong-ho had briefly appeased. Luckily, a short while later my wife woke up. Only then, when I realized how much better this was than if she'd woken up when I was there alone, did my mother-in-law's arrival come to seem like a good thing.

My mother-in-law came back, and was the first thing my wife's eyes fixed on. The older woman's face was wreathed in smiles from the moment she opened the door, whereas my wife's expression was difficult to decipher. She'd spent all day lying in bed and now, whether because of the drip or simply due to swelling, her face was practically bloodless, almost as white as milk.

Holding a steaming paper cup in one hand, my mother-in-law grasped my wife's hand in the other.

"This . . ." Her eyes welled with tears. "Take this. Ah, look at your face." My wife obediently took the paper cup. "It's herbal medicine. They say it strengthens the body. Why, in the old days, back before your marriage, we had the very same medicine made up for you, remember?"

My wife sniffed it and shook her head. "This isn't herbal medicine." Her expression cheerless and indifferent, and her eyes filled with something strangely like pity, my wife handed the cup back to her mother.

"It *is* herbal medicine. Just hold your nose and drink it down quickly."

"I'm not drinking it."

"Drink it. This is your mother's wish. Even the dead get their wishes obeyed, but you'd ignore your own mother's?"

She held the cup to my wife's lips.

"Is it really herbal medicine?"

"Of course, I just said so."

My wife held her nose and took a sip of the black liquid. My mother-in-law was all smiles, exclaiming, "More, drink more!" Her eyes flashed below their wrinkled lids.

"I'll keep it here and drink it a little later."

My wife lay back down again.

"What would you like to eat? Shall I buy something sweet to take away the aftertaste?"

"I'm all right."

All the same, the old woman kept on pestering me to go and find a shop. I refused to be harried into going, and eventually she left the room to find the shop herself. Then my wife pushed her blanket aside and got up.

"Where are you going?"

"The bathroom."

I picked up the IV bag and followed after her. She hung the bag up inside the toilet and locked the door. And then, accompanied by several groans, vomited up everything in her stomach.

She staggered out of the toilet, trailing the faint smell of gastric juices and the sour tang of semi-digested food. As I hadn't done it for her, she was forced to pick up her IV bag with her bandaged left hand, but she didn't hold it high enough and a small amount of blood began to flow back down the tube. Tottering forward, she picked up the bag of black goat her mother had set down by the bed. Her right hand, which clutched the heavy bag, still had the IV needle embedded in it, but she didn't pay this the slightest bit of notice. Then she left the ward—and I had absolutely no desire to go and find out what she was up to.

After a little while, the door banged loudly enough to make the schoolgirl and her mother frown in disapproval, and my mother-in-law burst in. She had a packet of cookies in one hand, and the paper shopping bag in the other—I could see even at a glance that the black liquid had burst out.

"Mr. Cheong, what on earth were you thinking of, just sitting there like that? Didn't you guess what that child might have been planning?"

More than anything else, I was strongly tempted just to walk out of the ward and go home.

"You, Yeong-hye, do you know how much this is worth? Would you throw it away? Money scraped together with your own parents' sweat and blood! How can you call yourself my daughter?"

The moment I saw my wife, bent at the waist, I noticed her red blood trickling backward into the IV bag.

"Look at yourself, now! Stop eating meat, and the world will devour you whole. Take a look in a mirror, go on, tell me what you look like!"

Finally, her high-pitched screeching subsided into low sobs. But my wife merely gazed at the sobbing woman as though she were a complete stranger, and eventually, as if having decided that this performance had gone on quite long enough, got back up onto the bed. She pulled the blanket up to her chest and closed her eyes. Only then did I raise the IV bag, now half full of crimson blood.

I don't know why that woman is crying. I don't know why she keeps staring at my face, either, as though she wants to swallow it. Or why she strokes the bandage on my wrist with her trembling hands.

My wrist is okay. It doesn't bother me. The thing that hurts is my chest. Something is stuck in my solar plexus. I don't know what it might be. It's lodged there permanently these days. Even though I've stopped wearing a bra, I can feel this lump all the time. No matter how deeply I inhale, it doesn't go away.

Yells and howls, threaded together layer upon layer, are enmeshed to form that lump. Because of meat. I ate too much meat. The lives of the animals I ate have all lodged there. Blood and flesh, all those butchered bodies are scattered in every nook and cranny, and though the physical remnants were excreted, their lives still stick stubbornly to my insides.

One time, just one more time, I want to shout. I want to throw myself through the pitch-black window. Maybe that would finally get this lump out of my body. Yes, perhaps that might work.

Nobody can help me. Nobody can save me. Nobody can make me breathe.

* * *

I packed my mother-in-law off in a taxi and when I got back the ward was dark. The schoolgirl and her mother, presumably fed up with all the commotion, had turned off the television and lights a little ahead of time, and drawn their curtain. My wife was sleeping. I lay down awkwardly on the cramped side bed and tried to fall asleep. I had absolutely no idea how I was going to sort this mess out. Only one thing was clear, and that was that this whole affair was bound to cause me no end of trouble.

When I eventually succeeded in falling asleep, I had a dream. In the dream, I was killing someone. I thrust a knife into their stomach with all my strength, then reached into the wound and wrenched out the long, coiled-up intestines. Like eating fish, I peeled off all the squishy flesh and muscle and left only the bones. But in the very instant I woke up, I ceased to remember who it was that I had killed.

It was early in the morning, still dark. Driven by a strange compulsion, I pulled back the blanket covering my wife. I fumbled in the pitch-black darkness, but there was no watery blood, no ripped intestines. I could hear the other patient's sleeping breath coming in little gasps, but my wife was unnaturally silent. I felt an odd trembling inside myself, and reached out with my index finger to touch her philtrum. She was alive.

When I woke up again the ward was already light.

"Goodness, you've been sleeping so deeply," the young girl's mother said. "You didn't even wake up when they came and brought the food." She sounded as though she felt rather sorry for me. I saw the meal tray that had been left on the bed. My wife hadn't even opened the rice bowl, had left the meal tray untouched, and gone . . . where? The IV had been pulled out too, and the bloody needle was dangling from the end of the long plastic tube.

"Where did she go?" I asked, wiping away the traces of drool from around my mouth.

"She was already gone when we woke up."

"What? In that case, you should have woken me, you know."

"Even if I'd tried to, you sleep like a log . . . of course, I would have woken you if it had seemed like something had happened." Her face reddened, either from anger or simple confusion.

I adjusted my clothes and rushed out, looking around impatiently as I passed down the corridor and came to the lift, but my wife was nowhere to be seen. I didn't have time for this. I'd told them at the office that I'd be two hours later than usual getting in; right now my wife should already have been being discharged. I decided that when I took her home I would tell her, and indeed myself, that we should just think of the whole thing as a bad dream.

I took the lift down to the ground floor. She wasn't in the lobby, so I hurried out into the hospital garden, out of breath but making sure to scan the area thoroughly. The only people in the garden were those patients who had already finished their breakfast. The early-morning chill, which would pass off soon enough, was fairly mild even now. You could tell who was a long-term patient based on how they looked—whether fatigued and gloomy, or peaceful. As I drew near the fountain, which was dry, I noticed that there was some kind of commotion; the people gathered there were all looking at something. I pushed my way through them until I had a clear view.

My wife was sitting on a bench by the fountain. She had removed her hospital gown and placed it on her knees, leaving her gaunt collarbones, emaciated breasts and brown nipples completely exposed. The bandage had been unwound from her left wrist, and the blood that was leaking out seemed to be slowly licking at the sutured area. Sunbeams bathed her face and naked body.

"How long has she been sitting there like that?"

"Good grief . . . she looks like she's come from the psychiatric ward, this young woman."

"What's that she's holding?"

"It looks like she's gripping something."

"Ah, look over there. They're coming now."

When I turned to look over my shoulder, a male nurse and a middle-aged guard could be seen hurrying over, their faces grave. I looked at my wife's exhausted face, her lips stained with blood like clumsily applied lipstick. Her eyes, which had been staring fixedly at the gathered audience, met mine. They glittered, as though filled with water.

I thought to myself: I do not know that woman. And it was true. It was not a lie. Nevertheless, and compelled by responsibilities that refused to be shirked, my legs carried me toward her, a movement that I could not for the life of me control.

"Darling, what are you doing?" I murmured in a low voice, picking up the hospital gown and using it to cover her bare chest.

"It's hot, so . . ." She smiled faintly—her familiar smile, a smile that could not have been more ordinary, and which I had believed I knew so well. "It's hot, so I just got undressed." She raised her left hand to shield her forehead from the streaming sunlight, revealing the cuts on her wrist.

"Have I done something wrong?"

I prized open her clenched right hand. A bird, which had been crushed in her grip, tumbled to the bench. It was a small white-eye bird, with feathers missing here and there. Below tooth marks that looked to have been caused by a predator's bite, vivid red bloodstains were spreading.

2

Mongolian Mark

The deep oxblood curtain fell over the stage. The dancers waved their hands so vigorously the whole row became a blur of movement, with individual figures impossible to make out. Though the applause was loud, with even the odd shout of "bravo" thrown in here and there, there was no curtain call. The ovation abruptly subsided and the audience began to gather up their bags and jackets and make their way to the aisles. He uncrossed his legs and stood up. He'd kept his arms folded during the five or so minutes of applause, silently gazing up at the dancers' eager faces as they greedily drank it in. Their efforts had inspired in him both compassion and respect, but the choreographer, he felt, hadn't deserved his applause.

He exited the auditorium and crossed the foyer, studying the now-obsolete performance posters. He'd been in a bookshop in the city center when he'd happened upon one of the posters, the sight of which had sent a shiver through his body. Worried that he might have missed the last performance, he'd hurriedly phoned the theater and made a reservation. On the poster, men and women sat displaying their naked backs, which were covered from the napes of their necks right down to their bottoms with flowers, coiling stems and thickly overlapping petals, painted on in red and blue. Looking at them he felt afraid, excited, and somehow oppressed. He couldn't believe that the image that had obsessed him for almost a year now had also been dreamed up by someone else—the choreographer—someone, moreover, whom he'd never even heard of. Was that image really about to unfold in front of him, just as he'd dreamed it? Sitting in his seat waiting for the lights to go down and the performance to start, he'd been so nervous he couldn't even take a sip of water.

But he hadn't found what he'd been looking for. Threading his way through the crowds of theatergoers who had thronged into the foyer, and who all looked so dazzling and extroverted, he headed for the exit nearest to the underground station. There had been nothing for him in the booming electronic music, the gaudy costumes, the showy nudity, or the overtly sexual gestures. The thing he'd been searching for was something quieter, deeper, more private.

He had to wait a while for a train, it being a Sunday afternoon, and when he got on he stood near the carriage door, holding a program with the photograph from the posters printed on its cover. His wife and five-year-old son were waiting at home. His wife, he knew, would have liked for them to spend weekends together as a family, but all the same he'd set aside a half day to see the performance. Would he get anything out of it? He'd known that, more than likely, he would only end up disillusioned yet again—that in the end, it was the only possible outcome. And now that was exactly what had happened. How on earth could a complete stranger be expected to tease out the inner logic of something he himself had dreamed up, to find a way to make it come alive? The bitterness that suddenly welled up inside him was exactly the same as the feeling he'd experienced a long time ago, on watching a video work by the Japanese artist Yayoi Kusama. The work had been filled with scenes of promiscuous sexual practices, featuring around ten men and women, each of them daubed all over with colored paint, their greed for each other's bodies playing out against a background of psychedelic music. They never stopped moving the whole time, flailing and floundering like fish out of water. Not that his own thirst was any less strong, of course— only he didn't want to express it like that. Anything but that.

After a while, the train went past the apartment complex where he lived. He'd never had any intention of getting off there. He stuffed the program into his backpack, rammed both fists into the pockets of his sweater, and studied the interior of the carriage as it was reflected in the window. He had to force himself to accept that the middle-aged man, who had a baseball cap concealing his receding hairline and a baggy sweater at least attempting to do the same for his paunch, was himself.

As luck would have it, the door to the studio was locked, which meant he had the place to himself. Sunday afternoons were practically the only times when he could use the space undisturbed. It was a small studio on the second floor below ground level of K group's headquarters, provided as part of their corporate sponsorship drive; the four video artists who shared the space had to take it in turns to use the single computer. He was grateful to be able to use the overhead equipment free of charge, but his sensitivity to the presence of others, which meant that he could only become properly absorbed in his work when he was alone, was a major stumbling block.

The door opened with a small click. He groped along the wall

until he found the light switch. Making sure to lock the door behind him first of all, he took off his cap and sweater, put his bag
down on the floor, then proceeded to pace up and down the narrow studio corridor for a while, his hands over his mouth, before
finally slumping down in front of the computer and putting his
head in his hands.

He opened his bag and got out the program, his sketchbook
and master tape. On that tape, which was labeled with his name,
address and phone number, were the originals of every video work
he'd made over the past ten years or so. It had already been two
years since he'd last stored a new work on the tape. Not that two
years was considered terminal as far as fallow periods went, but it
was still long enough to make him anxious.

He opened the sketchbook. The drawings filled scores of
pages and, despite being based on fundamentally the same idea,
were completely different from the performance poster in terms
of atmosphere and artistic feel. The naked bodies of the men and
women were brilliantly decorated, covered all over in painted
flowers, and there was something simple and straightforward
about the ways in which they were having sex. Without the taut
buttocks, tensed inner thighs, and the skinny upper bodies that
gave them a dancer's physique, there would have been no more
suggestiveness about them than there was with spring flowers.
Their bodies—he hadn't drawn in faces—had a stillness and so-
lidity that counterbalanced the arousing nature of the situation.

The image had come to him in a flash of inspiration. It had
happened last winter, when he'd started to believe that he might
somehow be able to bring his two-year-long fallow period to an
end, when he'd felt energy start to wriggle up from the pit of his
stomach, bit by bit. But how could he have known this energy

would coalesce into such a preposterous image? For one thing, up until then his work had always tended toward realism. And so, for someone who had previously worked on 3D graphics of people worn down by the vicissitudes of late capitalist society, to be screened as factual documentaries, the carnality, the pure sensuality of this image, was nothing short of monstrous.

And the image might never have come to him, if it hadn't been for a chance conversation. Had his wife not asked him to give their son a bath that Sunday afternoon. Had he not watched her helping their son to pull on his underpants after toweling him dry and been moved to exclaim, "That Mongolian mark is still so big! When on earth do they fade away?" Had she not replied thoughtlessly, "Well . . . I can't remember exactly when mine went. And Yeong-hye still had hers when she was twenty." If she hadn't then followed up his astonished *"Twenty?"* with "Mmm . . . just a thumb-sized thing, blue. And if she had it that long, who knows, maybe she's still got it now." In precisely that moment he was struck by the image of a blue flower on a woman's buttocks, its petals opening outward. In his mind, the fact that his sister-in-law still had a Mongolian mark on her buttocks became inexplicably bound up with the image of men and women having sex, their naked bodies completely covered with painted flowers. The causality linking these two things was so clear, so obvious, as to be somehow beyond comprehension, and thus it became etched into his mind.

Though her face was missing, the woman in his sketch was undoubtedly his sister-in-law. No, it *had* to be her. He'd imagined what her naked body must look like and began to draw, finishing it off with a dot like a small blue petal in the middle of her buttocks, and he'd got an erection. It was almost the first time since his marriage, and definitely the first time since he'd said good-bye to his mid-thirties, that he'd felt such intense sexual desire, a desire which, moreover, was focused on a clear object. And so who was the faceless man with his arms around her neck, looking as if he were attempting to throttle her, who was thrusting himself into her? He knew that it was himself; that, in fact, it could be none other. Arriving at this conclusion, he grimaced.

He spent a long time searching for a solution, for a way to free himself from the hold this image had on him, but nothing else would do as a substitute. Another image as intense and enticing as this one simply didn't exist. There was no other work he wanted to do. Every exhibition, film, performance, came to feel dull and flat, for no other reason than that it wasn't this.

He spent hours seemingly lost in a daydream, mulling over how to make the image become a reality. He would rent a studio from his painter friend and install lighting, get some body paints and a white sheet to cover the floor . . . he let his thoughts run on like this even though the most important thing, persuading his sister-in-law, still remained to be done. He agonized for a long time over whether he might be able to replace her with another woman, when the suspicion occurred to him, somewhat belatedly, that the film he was planning could all too easily be categorized as pornography. Never mind his sister-in-law, no woman would agree to such a thing. In that case, should he shell out a large sum of money to hire a professional actress? Even if, after making a hundred concessions, he eventually managed to get the thing filmed, would he really be able to exhibit it? He'd often anticipated that his work, which dealt with social issues, might put him in the firing line with some people, but never before had he imagined himself being branded as some peddler of cheap titillation. He'd always been completely unrestricted when it came to making his art, and so it hadn't ever really occurred to him that this freedom might become a luxury.

If it hadn't been for the image he would never have had to go through all this anxiety, this discomfort and unease, this agonizing doubt and self-examination. He wouldn't have had to suffer the fear of losing everything he'd achieved—not that that really amounted to all that much—even his family, in one fell swoop, and due to a choice that he himself had made. He was becoming divided against himself. Was he a normal human being? More than that, a moral human being? A strong human being, able to control his own impulses? In the end, he found himself unable to claim with any certainty that he knew the answers to these questions, though he'd been so sure before.

He heard the click of keys in the lock, quickly covered the sketchbook and turned to face the door. Whoever it was, he didn't want his drawings to catch his or her eye. This was something new and a little strange for him. He never usually held back when it came to showing his sketches or concepts to other people.

"Hey!" It was J, his long hair tied back in a ponytail. "I didn't think there was anyone in here."

He leaned back, keeping his movements deliberately slow, and laughed.

"Fancy a cup of coffee?" J asked, fishing some coins out of his pocket.

He shook his head. While J went to get a coffee from the vending machine, he looked around the studio, now no longer his own private space. He put his baseball cap back on, uncomfortable at the thought of his balding crown being on show. Like a cough that tickles the throat, he could feel a long-suppressed yell threatening to burst out from deep inside him. He swept his things into his bag and fled the studio, hurrying toward the lift. In his reflection in the lift's door, which gleamed like a mirror, it looked as though tears were streaming from his bloodshot eyes. However much he combed his memory, he couldn't recall anything like this having happened to him before. Right at that moment, he wanted nothing more than to spit at those red, lined eyes. He wanted to pummel his cheeks until the blood showed through beneath his black beard, and smash his ugly lips, swollen with desire, with the sole of his shoe.

"You're late," his wife said, making an effort not to sound too put out. Their son turned back to the plastic forklift truck he'd been playing with. It was impossible to tell whether or not he was glad to see his father.

Since his wife had gone back to working full-time at her cosmetics store, she was constantly exhausted, but she was the type to press on regardless, diligent and persevering. Practically the only thing she asked of him was to keep Sunday daytimes free. "I'd like to have a bit of a rest myself . . . and our son needs to spend time with his father too, doesn't he?" He knew that this was the only time of the week she would allow herself a bit of a break. She was even grateful that he let her take on so much responsibility, running a business as well as a household, without so much as a word of complaint. But these days, every time he looked at her he saw her sister's face overlaid on hers, and their domestic life couldn't have been further from his thoughts.

"Have you had dinner?"

"Yeah, I grabbed something on the way."

"You have to eat properly, why do you always just grab something on the go?" Her tone was resigned, as though she'd long given her husband up as a lost cause. He examined her exhausted-looking face the way one might look at a complete stranger. Her eyes were deep and clear, framed by naturally double eyelids, and her face was a slender oval, with a smooth, feminine jawline. The success of the cosmetics store, which had expanded over the years from the two-and-a-half-p'yong space which she'd somehow managed to set up when she was still a young girl, must have been largely down to the impression of affability which these pleasant, open features gave. And yet, right from the first there'd been something about her that left him feeling vaguely dissatisfied. Her face, figure and thoughtful nature all combined to form the spitting image of the woman he'd spent so long trying to find; and so, unable to put his finger on just what it was that he felt she was lacking, he'd made up his mind to marry her. In fact, it was only when he was introduced to her sister that he realized what it was his new wife was missing.

Everything about her sister pleased him—her single-lidded eyes; the way she spoke, so blunt as to be almost uncouth, and without his wife's faintly nasal inflection; her drab clothes; her androgynously protruding cheekbones. She might well be called ugly in comparison with his wife, but to him she radiated energy, like a tree that grows in the wilderness, denuded and solitary. All the same, he felt no different toward her than he had before they'd met. "Huh, now *she's* my type; even though they're sisters, and they're quite similar in many ways, there's some subtle difference between them"—this thought flitted briefly through his mind, and was gone.

"Shall I make you something to eat or not?" His wife's question was almost a demand.

"I told you, I've already eaten."

Exhausted from all the emotions roiling inside him, he opened the bathroom door. As soon as he turned the light on, his wife's voice drilled into his ears once more.

"On top of everything else, I'm worried about Yeong-hye; I didn't hear from you all day, and Ji-woo has a cold so I had to stay with him all the time . . ." Her sigh was followed by a shout directed at their son. "What are you doing? I told you to come and take your medicine!" Knowing that the boy would dawdle, his wife slowly poured the powdered medicine onto a spoon and mixed it with a strawberry-colored syrup. He emerged from the bathroom and closed the door behind him.

"What about your sister?" he asked his wife. "What's happened now?"

"She finally got served with the divorce papers, of course! It's not that I don't understand Mr. Cheong's position, but all the same, he could have shown a bit more sympathy. To just throw away a marriage like that . . ."

"I . . . ," he stammered. "Shall I call around and see her?"

His wife suddenly became animated. "Would you? We haven't had her around in such a long time, and if you were to go and see her, even if it's a bit awkward . . . but you know, it's not as though she doesn't understand the difficulty. She knows that's just how things turned out." He studied his wife, a picture of responsible compassion as she carefully approached their son with the medicine. She's a good woman, he thought. The kind of woman whose goodness is oppressive.

"I'll give her a call tomorrow."

"Do you need the number?"

"No, I've got it."

Feeling as though his chest might be about to burst, he went back inside the bathroom and closed the door. He turned on the shower and listened to the water drumming down into the bathtub as he took off his clothes. He was aware that he hadn't had sex with his wife for close on two months. But he also knew that his penis's sudden rigidity was nothing to do with her.

He'd pictured to himself his sister-in-law's rented studio apartment, the one she'd shared with his wife back when they were young, pictured her curled up there on the bed, then switched to remembering how it had felt to carry her on his back, her body pressed up against his and staining his clothes with her blood, the feel of her chest and buttocks, imagined himself pulling down her trousers just enough to reveal the blue brand of the Mongolian mark.

He stood there and masturbated. A moan escaped from between his lips, not quite laughter and not quite a sob. The shock of the too-cold water.

It had been the beginning of summer two years ago when his sister-in-law had cut her wrist open in his house. They'd moved there only recently, wanting the extra floor space, and his wife's family had all come around for lunch. He'd heard about his sister-in-law apparently turning vegetarian, something that hadn't sat at all well with this family of meat lovers, the father in particular. She'd been so pitifully thin, it wasn't as though he couldn't understand them giving her a strict dressing-down. But that her father, the Vietnam War hero, had actually struck his rebellious daughter in the face and physically forced a lump of meat into her mouth, that was something else. However much he thought back on it, he couldn't convince himself that it had actually happened—it was more like a scene from some bizarre play.

More vivid and frightening than any other was the memory of the scream that had erupted from his sister-in-law when the lump of meat approached her lips. After spitting it out, she'd snatched up the fruit knife and glared fiercely at each of her family in turn, her terrified eyes rolling like those of a cornered animal.

Once the blood was gushing out of her wrist he'd torn a strip from one of their quilts, bound it around her wrist and picked her up, her body so light she could almost have been a ghost. As he ran down to the car park, he'd been surprised by the speed and decisiveness of his own actions, something he'd never before real- ized he was capable of.

As he watched her unconscious form receive emergency medi- cal treatment, he'd heard a sound like something snapping inside his own body. The feeling he'd had at that moment was one that, even now, he found himself unable to explain with any degree of accuracy. A person had attacked her own body right in front of his eyes, tried to hack at it like it was a piece of meat; her blood had soaked his white shirt, mingling with his sweat and gradually drying to a dark brown stain.

He remembered hoping she would survive, but at the same time doubting just what that "survival" would mean. The moment she'd tried to take her own life had been a turning point. Now there was nothing anyone could do to help her. Every single one of them—her parents who had force-fed her meat, her husband and siblings who had stood by and let it happen—were distant strangers, if not actual enemies. If she woke up again, that situation wouldn't have changed. Just because this suicide attempt had been spur-of-the-moment didn't mean she wouldn't try it again. And if she did, no doubt she'd be more careful in how she went about it, and that meant there mightn't be anyone to stop her as there had been this time. All of a sudden he became aware of the conclusion his thoughts had led him to: that it would be better if she didn't wake up, that if she did the situation would actually be ambiguous, ghastly, that perhaps he ought to throw her out of the window while her eyes were still closed.

Once she was out of danger, he'd used the money her husband had given him to go to a shop and buy a new shirt to change into. Instead of throwing away his soiled shirt, which stank of blood, he'd bundled it up into a ball and taken it with him in the taxi home. During the journey, his most recent video work had come to mind, and he'd been surprised to find himself recalling it as something that had caused him unbearable pain. The work was based around images related to things he loathed and thought of as lies, edited together into an impressionistic montage with music and graphic subtitles: ads, clips from the news and television dramas, politicians' faces, ruined bridges and department stores, vagrants, and the tears of children who suffered from incurable diseases.

He had felt suddenly sick. Even though those images had undeniably caused him agony, even though he'd hated them, the individual moments contained in the work, which he'd stayed up all night wrestling with, struggling to face up to the true nature of the emotions they provoked in him, had now come to feel like a form of violence. At that moment his thoughts crossed a boundary, and he wanted to fling open the door of the speeding taxi and tumble out onto the tarmac. He could no longer bear the thought of those images, of the reality they portrayed. Back then, when he *had* been able to deal with them, it must have been because his hatred of them was somehow underdeveloped—or else because he hadn't been sufficiently threatened by them. But just then, shut up inside the taxi that sweltering summer afternoon with the smell of his sister-in-law's blood assailing his nostrils, those images and that reality were suddenly threatening, making the bile rise in his throat and the breath catch in his lungs. It occurred to him that it might be a long time before he was capable of making another work. He was worn out, and life revolted him. He couldn't cope with all these things it contaminated.

The past ten or so years' worth of work was quietly turning its back on him. It wasn't his anymore. It belonged to a person he used to know, or thought he'd known—once upon a time.

His sister-in-law was silent on the other end of the phone. He knew she was there, though; he could hear a faint sighing sound, like breathing, overlaid with a kind of rattling that he guessed was coming from the line.

"Hello?" He was finding it difficult to force the words out. "Sister-in-law, it's me. Ji-woo's mum is . . ." He despised himself, all his hypocrisy and trickery, but fought this down and continued speaking. "Well, she's worried, you know."

Still no answer. He sighed into the receiver. She would be standing there barefoot, he knew, like always. When her time at the psychiatric hospital, where she'd spent several months, had come to a close, she'd come to stay with them while his wife and the rest of the family all went to try to persuade her husband to take her back. The month she'd spent with them, before moving out into a rented studio apartment, had caused none of them even the slightest strain. Partly this was because he had yet to hear about the Mongolian mark, and thus regarded her as nothing more than an object of pity, albeit a faintly inscrutable one.

She'd never been much of a talker, and had spent the majority of her time out on their veranda, sunning herself in the late-autumn sunshine. She would occupy herself in picking up the dried leaves that had fallen from the flowerpots and crumbling them into a fine powder, or in stretching out the palm of her hand to cast shadows over the floor. When his wife was busy with something she would lend a hand with Ji-woo, taking him to the bathroom and helping him wash, her bare feet kissing the cold tiles.

It was difficult to believe that such a woman had once tried to kill herself, or that she'd sat topless in front of a crowd of strangers, perfectly composed, which had apparently been a symptom of some kind of post-suicide-attempt dementia. That he had run to the hospital with her bleeding on his back, and that the experience had had such a profound effect on him, seemed like something that had happened with a different woman, or perhaps in a different time.

The only thing that was especially unusual about her was that she didn't eat meat. This had been a source of friction with her family from the start, and since her behavior after this initial change had grown increasingly strange—culminating in her wandering around topless—her husband had decided that her vegetarianism was proof that she would never be "normal" again.

"She was always so submissive—outwardly, at any rate. And for a woman who wasn't quite all there to start with to be taking medication every day, well, she's bound to get worse, and that's all there is to it."

What threw him was the way that his brother-in-law seemed to consider it perfectly natural to discard his wife as though she were a broken watch or household appliance.

"Now don't go making me out to be some kind of villain. Anyone can see that I'm the real victim here."

Unable to deny that there was at least a measure of truth in this, he, unlike his wife, kept a neutral position on the matter. She, on the other hand, begged Mr. Cheong to hold off on the formal divorce proceedings and wait to see how things would pan out, but he remained unmoved.

He made an effort to push Mr. Cheong's face out of his mind, that narrow forehead, pointed jaw and general look of stubbornness which he'd always found unpleasant. He tried speaking Yeong-hye's name again.

"Answer me, sister-in-law. Whatever you say, just answer." Just as he thought there was nothing else for it but to hang up, she spoke.

"The water's boiling." Her voice had no weight to it, like feathers. It was neither gloomy nor absentminded, as might be expected of someone who was ill. But it wasn't bright or light-hearted either. It was the quiet tone of a person who didn't belong anywhere, someone who had passed into a border area between states of being.

"I'll have to go and turn it off."

"Sister-in-law, I . . ." He spoke hurriedly, panicking that she might put the phone down and cut him off. "Is it okay if I come over now? You aren't going out anywhere today?"

After a brief silence, he heard a click and the tone which signaled that the call had been ended. He put down the phone, his hand slick with sweat.

* * *

It was clearly only after hearing about her Mongolian mark from his wife that he'd started to see his sister-in-law in a new light. Before that, he'd never had any kind of ulterior motive when it came to his dealings with her. When he recalled how she'd looked and acted during the time she'd spent living with them, the sexual desire that flooded through him was a product of his mental re-enactment of these past experiences, not something he'd actually felt at the time. He felt his skin grow heated every time he called to mind her absentminded expression as she sat on the veranda throwing out shadows with her hand, the flash of white ankle that her baggy tracksuit bottoms had revealed while she was help-ing his son to wash, the nonchalant line of her body as she'd sat sprawled in front of the television, her half-naked legs, her disheveled hair. And stamped over all these memories was the blue Mon-golian mark—that mark which appeared on the buttocks or backs of children, usually fading away long before adulthood.

Now, the fact that she didn't eat meat, only vegetables and ce-real grains, seemed to fit with the image of that blue petal-like mark, so much so that the one could not be disentangled from the other, and the fact that the blood that had gushed out of her artery had soaked his white shirt, drying into the dark, matte bur-gundy of red bean soup, felt like a shocking, indecipherable pre-monition of his own eventual fate.

Her room was in a fairly quiet alley near to a women's uni-versity. He stood in front of the multistory building, laden down with two big bags of fruit that his wife had insisted he bring with him—tangerines, pears and apples from Jeju Island, and even some out-of-season strawberries. The knotted muscles in his hands and arms ached, but still he stood there wavering, realizing as he did that the thought of going up to her apartment, of encountering her in person, was making him afraid.

At last he set the fruit down, flipped open his mobile and dialed her number. When she still hadn't answered after the tenth ring, he picked the fruit up again and began to climb the stairs. When he reached the third floor he went over to the corner apartment and pressed the doorbell, which had a picture of a semiquaver. Just as he'd thought: no answer. He tried turning the handle. To his surprise, the door opened. He readjusted his baseball cap, only then realizing that his hair was soaked with sweat, tidied himself up a bit, took a deep breath, and pushed the door.

The south-facing studio apartment was bathed in the early-October sunlight as far in as the kitchen area, and felt still. Some of his wife's clothes, which she'd passed on to her sister, were lying scattered across the floor, and there were tiny dust balls rolling about, but somehow the place managed not to seem untidy. Perhaps that was because of the almost complete lack of furniture.

After putting the fruit down next to the door, he took off his shoes and went in. There was no sign of her anywhere. Perhaps she'd gone out. Perhaps she'd gone out deliberately because he'd told her he was coming. There was no television, and there was something unseemly about the way the two wall sockets, next to the hole for an antenna, lay exposed in the middle of the wall. At the far end of the living room–cum–bedroom, where his wife had installed a solitary telephone, there was a mattress, on top of which the quilt was rumpled up into a cave-like mound, as though someone had just slid out from under it.

The air felt stale, and he was on the point of opening the door to the veranda when he heard a noise and whipped around. The breath caught in his throat.

She was coming out of the bathroom. The real shock, though, was that she was naked. She stood there blankly for a moment, as though she, too, were somewhat startled, and without the slightest trace of moisture visible on her naked body. But then she began to pick up the scattered clothes one by one and slip them on. She did this quite calmly, not in the least flustered or embarrassed, as though getting dressed were merely something demanded by the situation, rather than something she herself felt to be necessary.

While she stood there getting dressed, calmly and methodically and without turning her back to him, he was of course aware that he should either avert his gaze or hurry outside. And yet he remained standing there, as if rooted to the spot. She wasn't as gaunt as when she'd initially turned vegetarian. She'd gradually put on weight after being admitted to the hospital, and she'd eaten well when she'd been staying with him and his wife, thanks to which her breasts had now rounded out into softness. Her waist narrowed sharply, her body hair was fairly sparse, and the overall effect, aside from the line of her thigh, which he felt could have done with being a little rounder, was one of an enticing lack of superfluity. Rather than provoking lust, it was a body that made one want to rest one's gaze quietly upon it. Once she'd finished sorting through the clothes and putting them on she came up to him, and it occurred to him that he hadn't managed to get a look at her Mongolian mark.

"I'm sorry." Belatedly he stammered his excuse. "What with the door being open, I thought you'd just popped out for something or other."

"It's okay." Now, too, she spoke as though answering like this was the expected, necessary thing. "It's just that I enjoy being like this when I'm on my own."

So. He tried to collect his thoughts; his mind had gone blank. She's saying that she always walks around with her clothes off in the house. He'd been fine just a moment ago when confronted with her naked body, but as soon as he grasped what she was saying he became flustered and felt his penis becoming engorged. He took off his baseball cap and squatted down awkwardly, trying to conceal his erection.

"I've nothing to offer you to eat . . ."

She walked over to the kitchen area and he took in the fact that her light gray tracksuit bottoms were grazing her bare skin, knowing from what he'd just seen that she wasn't wearing anything underneath. Her buttocks were neither large nor particularly voluptuous. Nothing to account for why his mouth was suddenly so dry.

"I'm not really hungry," he said, stalling for time in the hope he'd be able to suppress his arousal. "How about we just eat some of this fruit?"

"If you like." She went over to the front door, picked up the pears and apples and carried them to the sink. Listening to the sound of running water and the clinking of dishes, he tried to concentrate on the ugly electrical sockets and the angular telephone buttons, but the memory of her pubic region only intensified in his mind. His head throbbed with the image of her buttocks crowded with colored petals, overlying that of the man and woman having sex, with which he'd covered page after page of his sketchbook.

When she came and sat down next to him, carrying plates of

the peeled, sliced fruit, he had to bow his head so that she wouldn't see the look in his eyes.

"I don't know if the apples will be any good . . ." He trailed off.

After a while, she broke the silence. "You know, you don't have to come and visit me."

"Oh?"

"The doctor said I wasn't to do any kind of job where I would be left alone with my own thoughts," she continued in a low voice, "so I'm thinking of trying somewhere like a department store. I even had an interview last week."

"Really?"

This was surprising. "Would *you* be able to put up with a wife who was always like that, zoned out on psychiatric medication every day, completely dependent on you for her livelihood?" This was something Mr. Cheong had said to him during one of their phone calls, slurring as if he were drunk. Now it turned out that prediction had been off; she wasn't as far gone as all that. Turning his upper body toward her, though with his eyes still fixed on the ground, he finally got to the point.

"How about working at your sister's store instead?" As he carried on talking he felt his arousal subside a little. "Ji-woo's mum pays a decent wage—you know what a good person she is—and she'd much rather see it go to you than to a stranger. She's your sister, which means you can trust each other, and she'd like for the two of you to spend more time together. Besides, the work wouldn't be as tough as at a department store."

Slowly she turned to face him, and he saw that her expression was as serene as that of a Buddhist monk. Such uncanny serenity actually frightened him, making him think that perhaps this was a surface impression left behind after any amount of unspeakable viciousness had been digested, or else settled down inside her as a kind of sediment. He reproached himself for having used her as a kind of mental pornography, when she simply had an innocent wish to be naked. All the same, he was unable to deny that the image of her naked was now stamped indelibly on his brain, burned into him like a brand.

"Have some pear." She held the plate out to him.

"You have some too."

Using her fingers instead of a fork, she picked up a piece of pear and put it in her mouth. He averted his head, frightened by the sudden urge he had to throw his arms around her still form—so still in fact she appeared to be lost in thought—to suck on her index finger, sticky with sweet pear juice, and lick the last of the juice from her lips and tongue, and to pull her baggy tracksuit bottoms down right then and there.

"It'll only take a minute," he said, slipping his feet into his shoes. "You'll come with me?"

"Where to?"

"We could just walk around, talk for a bit."

"I'll try and think of something that might interest you."

"No, no, there's no need . . . the thing is, I have a favor to ask."

She looked unsure, but he'd already made up his mind. If he was to escape from this agonizing situation, the inexplicable compulsions that were gradually taking him over, he needed to get outside, out of this room. It was too dangerous for him to stay there a moment longer.

"We can talk here."

"No, I want to walk for a bit. Besides, isn't it stifling for you to be cooped up inside all day?"

Eventually, as though resigned to having lost this argument, she put on her slippers and followed him out. They walked down the alley without speaking to each other, and continued along the main road. When he spotted a sign for a chain café he asked her, "Do you like shaved ice?" She gave a half smile, looking for all the world like a girl on a date who doesn't want to seem too easily pleased.

The two of them took a seat by the window. He looked across at her in silence as she mixed red bean into the shaved ice slush and licked it from the tip of her wooden spoon. As if there were a wire linking her tongue with his body, every time that little pink tip darted out he found himself flinching as though from an electric shock.

And he thought to himself that perhaps there was only one way out. That perhaps the only way out of this hell of desire would be to make those images into a reality.

"So, the favor . . ."

She fixed him with her glance, a dot of red bean on the tip of her tongue. In her single-lidded eyes, the simple line of which made her look almost Mongolian, her pupils, which were neither large nor small, shone with a faint light.

"I'd like you to model for me."

She neither laughed nor became flustered. She kept her calm gaze fixed on him, as if intending to bore inside.

"You've been to some of my exhibitions, right?"

"Yes."

"It'll be a video work, similar to my other ones. And it won't take long. You just have to . . . take your clothes off." Now that he'd finally come out and said it he felt suddenly bold, and was sure that his hands, which had already stopped sweating, would also become steadier. His forehead felt cooler too. "You'll take your clothes off, and I'll paint your body." Her eyes, calm as ever, still gazed across at his.

"You'll paint on me?"

"That's right. You'll keep the paint on until the filming is over."

"Paint . . . on my body?"

"I'm going to paint flowers." Her eyes seemed to flicker. Perhaps he'd made a mistake. "It won't be difficult. An hour, maybe two—that's all I'll need. Whenever's convenient for you."

Having said all that there was to say, he lowered his head with an air of resignation and examined his ice cream. Topped with crushed peanuts and flaked almonds, it was slowly melting, the liquid pooling around the sides.

"Where?"

His mind was on the melting ice cream, which was beginning to turn to froth, when this question finally came. He looked up to find her spooning the last of her shaved ice into her mouth, its redness smeared over her bloodless lips.

"I'm planning on renting a friend's studio." Her face was so utterly devoid of expression, it was impossible for him to guess what was going on inside her mind. "Ah . . . your sister . . ." He wished he didn't have to bring this up, but there seemed to be no way around it; his stammering words seemed to betray him, showing him the situation for what it really was in a flash of painful clarity. "You see . . . it's a secret."

She gave no sign of assent, but none of refusal either. He held his breath and greedily scanned her impassive features, desperate to fathom the answer that she meant this silence to signify.

M's studio was pleasantly warm, thanks to the wide window that allowed the sunlight to stream in. The space was around a hundred p'yong, more like the size of an art gallery than a studio. M's paintings were hung up in carefully chosen spots, and his painting materials were all arranged in a surprisingly ordered fashion, so much so that he found himself tempted to try them out even though he'd already put together sufficient paints and brushes of his own.

"I was quite surprised when you called me up," M had said, when he was handing him the keys after making him a cup of tea. M had managed to secure a full-time post at a Seoul university at only thirty-two, the first from their graduating class to do so, and now his face, clothes and attitude all combined to endow him with the dignity of a professor. "If you ever want to borrow the studio again, please just ask. I spend most mornings and afternoons at the school, so it's usually free then."

He took down a few of M's paintings, the ones that were slightly overlapping the edges of the window, thinking as he did so that they were far more conventional than anything he would put his name to. He spread a white sheet over the large rectangle of wooden floor upon which the light fell most strongly, and lay down upon it for a while, checking what she would have in her field of vision and whether the position would feel comfortable enough. The wooden beams spanning the high ceiling, the sky outside the window, the sheet, a layer of softness between his back and the hard floor, which was a little chilly but not unbearably so.

He turned over onto his front, where different things caught his eye: M's pictures, the patch of sunlight carved into the shade of the wooden floor, the soot caked onto the unused brick stove.

He spread out his painting materials, checked the batteries in his PD100 camcorder, set up the studio lighting for a long session of filming, opened his sketchbook, closed it again, put it back in his bag, took off his sweater, rolled up his sleeves, and waited. When it was getting on for three p.m., which was when they'd arranged to meet, he pulled his sweater back on and put on his shoes. He walked briskly to the underground station, breathing in the clean air of the suburbs.

His mobile rang, and he kept walking while he answered the call.

"It's me." His wife. "It looks like I'm going to be late finishing today. And the babysitter's got a flat tire. You'll have to pick Ji-woo up from the nursery at seven."

"I can't," he answered shortly. "I can do nine at the earliest." He heard his wife sigh.

"All right. I'll ask the woman in 709 to look after him until nine."

They hung up without any unnecessary small talk. That was the kind of relationship they had these days—that of business partners who were careful to excise any superfluity from their dealings, and whose only shared business was their child.

That night a few days ago after he'd gone to see his sister-in-law, he'd reached out in the darkness and pulled his wife to him, without giving himself time to think about what he was doing. Surprised and confused by this apparent show of desire, his wife still had no reason to question that this was what it was. If she'd looked, she would have seen something closer to fear in her husband's eyes. But it was dark.

"What's got into you?" He'd put his hand over her mouth then, so he wouldn't have to hear that nasal voice. He pushed himself toward the image of *her*, finding it there in his wife's nose and lips, the child-like curve of her neck, all outlined vaguely in the darkness. With her nipple standing straight and hard in his mouth, he reached down and pulled off her knickers. Every time he wanted to get the image of the small blue petal to open and close, he shut his eyes and tried to block out his wife's face.

When it was all over, she was crying. He couldn't tell what these tears meant—pain, pleasure, passion, disgust, or some inscrutable loneliness that she would have been no more able to explain than he would have been to understand. He didn't know.

I'm scared, she'd muttered, turned away from him. No, it wasn't that. *You're scaring me.* At that point he was already slipping into a death-like sleep, so he couldn't be sure if those words had really passed his wife's lips. She might have lain there sobbing for hours in the darkness. He didn't know.

But the next morning she hadn't acted any different from usual. On the phone just now, there'd been no trace in her voice of what had happened between them, no particular sense of hostility toward him. It was just that her way of speaking—that almost inhuman patience, those trademark sighs of hers—made him feel incredibly uncomfortable. He walked a little faster, trying to shake that feeling off.

Surprisingly, his sister-in-law was already waiting at the station exit, slumped on the steps as if she'd been there a long time. Wearing a fairly chunky brown sweater over shabby jeans, she seemed to have stepped straight out of another season. He stared at her face, which was shiny with sweat, and ran his eyes over the contours of her body. He stood there for a while without calling out to her, wanting to keep her there in freeze-frame. Passersby flicked uneasy glances toward this man who looked possessed.

"Take off your clothes," he said in a low voice.

She was standing staring blankly at the white poplars outside the window. The afternoon sunlight shone desolate on the white sheet. She didn't turn around. Thinking she hadn't heard him, he was on the point of repeating himself when she raised her arms and pulled her sweater up over her head. The white T-shirt she had on underneath came off next, exposing her naked back; she wasn't wearing a bra. She slipped off her old jeans and revealed her two white buttocks.

He held his breath and examined them. Above were the pair of dimpled hollows commonly called "the angel's smile." The birthmark was thumb sized, imprinted on the upper left buttock. How could such a thing still be there after all these years? It didn't make any sense. Its pale blue-green resembled that of a faint bruise, but it was clearly a Mongolian mark. It called to mind something ancient, something pre-evolutionary, or else perhaps a mark of photosynthesis, and he realized to his surprise that there was nothing at all sexual about it; it was more vegetal than sexual.

Only after some time did he tear his eyes away from the Mongolian mark and consider her naked body in its entirety. Her composure was impressive considering that she wasn't a professional model, and taking into account the kind of relationship she'd had with her now ex-husband. Suddenly he remembered being told how she'd been found stripped to the waist in front of the hospital fountain, that day when she slit her wrist; that that was what had led to her being put in a closed ward; that her discharge had been delayed because even in the hospital she kept trying to take her clothes off and expose herself to the sunlight.

"Should I sit down?" she asked.

"No, lie on your stomach," he told her, his voice so low it was barely intelligible. She did as he said. He stood there completely motionless, frowning as he struggled to identify the source of the roiling confusion inside him, which the sight of her prone body had stirred up. "Stay just like that. Give me a minute to set up."

He fixed the camcorder to the tripod and adjusted the height. Once he'd arranged it so that her prone body filled the frame exactly, he got out his paints, his palette and brushes. He'd decided to film himself painting her.

First he swept up the hair that was falling over her shoulders, and then, starting from the nape of her neck, he began to paint. Half-open buds, red and orange, bloomed splendidly on her shoulders and back, and slender stems twined down her side. When he reached the hump of her right buttock he painted an orange flower in full bloom, with a thick, vivid yellow pistil protruding from its center. He left the left buttock, the one with the Mongolian mark, undecorated. Instead, he just used a large brush to cover the area around the bluish mark with a wash of light green, fainter than the mark itself, so that the latter stood out like the pale shadow of a flower.

Every time the brush swept over her skin he felt her flesh quiver delicately as if being tickled, and he shuddered. But it

92 Han Kang

wasn't arousal; rather, it was a feeling that stimulated something deep in his very core, passing through him like a continuous electric shock.

By the time he eventually completed the leaves and long stems, which continued over her right thigh all the way down to her slender ankle, he was completely drenched with sweat.

"All done," he said. "Just stay like that for a minute more."

He took the camera off the tripod and began to film her close up. He zoomed in on the details of each flower, and made a long collage of the curve of her neck, her disheveled hair, her two hands resting on the sheet, seeming tense, and the buttock with the Mongolian mark. Once he'd finally captured her whole body on the tape, he switched off the camcorder.

"You can get up now."

Fairly worn out, he sat down on the sofa in front of the brick stove. She rested her elbows on the floor, raising herself up slowly as though her limbs were stiff and aching.

"Aren't you cold?" He wiped away his sweat, stood up and spread his sweater over her shoulders. "It wasn't difficult for you?"

This time she looked at him and laughed. Her laughter was faint but lively, seeming to reject nothing and be surprised by nothing.

Only then did he realize what it was that had shocked him when he'd first seen her lying prone on the sheet. This was the body of a beautiful young woman, conventionally an object of desire, and yet it was a body from which all desire had been eliminated. But this was nothing so crass as carnal desire, not for her—rather, or so it seemed, what she had renounced was the very life that her body represented. The sunlight that came splintering through the wide window, dissolving into grains of sand, and the beauty of that body that, though this was not visible to the eye, was also ceaselessly splintering . . . the overwhelming inexpressibility of the scene beat against him like a wave breaking on the rocks, alleviating even those terrifyingly unknowable compulsions that had caused him such pain over the past year.

She put on her jeans and his sweater, and wrapped her hands around a mug from which the steam was rising. She left her slippers by the door, stepping lightly across the floor in her bare feet.

"It wasn't cold?" he asked for the second time, and she shook her head. "And it wasn't difficult?"

"All I did was lie there. And the floor was warm."

The whole situation was undeniably bizarre, yet she displayed an almost total lack of curiosity, and indeed it seemed that this was what enabled her to maintain her composure no matter what she was faced with. She made no move to investigate the unfamiliar space, and showed none of the emotions that one might expect. It seemed enough for her to just deal with whatever it was that came her way, calmly and without fuss. Or perhaps it was simply that things were happening inside her, terrible things, which no one else could even guess at, and thus it was impossible for her to engage with everyday life at the same time. If so, she would naturally have no energy left, not just for curiosity or interest but indeed for any meaningful response to all the humdrum minutiae that went on on the surface. What suggested to him that this might be the case was that, on occasion, her eyes would seem to reflect a kind of violence that could not simply be dismissed as passivity or idiocy or indifference, and which she would appear to be struggling to suppress. Just then she was staring down at her feet, her hands wrapped around the mug, shoulders hunched like a baby chick trying to get warm. And yet she didn't look at all pitiful sitting there; instead, it made her appear uncommonly hard and self-contained, so much so that anyone watching would feel uneasy, and want to look away.

He recalled the face of her ex-husband, whom he'd never liked, and whom he no longer had any need to call "brother-in-law." A dry face, which seemed to value nothing outside of the every-day, nothing he couldn't touch with his own two hands; the mere thought of those vulgar lips pressed greedily against her body, those lips that had never mouthed anything other than the trite and conventional, filled him with a kind of shame. Did that insen-sitive oaf know about her Mongolian mark? He couldn't imagine their naked bodies twined together without its seeming insulting, and defiling, and violent.

She stood up, holding out the empty cup, and so he stood up too. He took the cup and put it down on the table. He then re-placed the tape in the camcorder and readjusted the tripod.

"Shall we go again?" She nodded and walked over to the sheet. The sunlight was now a little weaker than before, so he turned on one of the overhead tungsten lights, the one directly over the sheet.

She shed her clothes and lay down again, on her back this time, looking up at the ceiling. The spotlighting made him narrow his eyes as if dazzled, although the upper half of her body was still in shadow. Of course, he'd seen her naked body front-on before, when he'd accidentally disturbed her in her apartment, but the sight of her lying there utterly without resistance, yet armored by the power of her own renunciation, was so intense as to bring tears to his eyes. Her skinny collarbones; her breasts that, because she was lying on her back, were slender and elongated like those of a young girl; her visible ribcage; her parted thighs, their position incongruously unsexual; her face, still and swept clean, open eyes which could well have been asleep. It was a body from which all superfluity had gradually been whittled away. Never before had he set eyes on such a body, a body that said so much and yet was no more than itself.

This time he painted huge clusters of flowers in yellow and white, covering the skin from her collarbone to her breasts. If the flowers on her back were the flowers of the night, these were the brilliant flowers of the day. Orange day lilies bloomed on her concave stomach, and golden petals were scattered pell-mell over her thighs.

A thrilling energy seemed to flow out quietly from some unknowable place inside his body and collect on the tip of his brush. He wanted only to draw it out for as long as possible. The light from the tungsten lamp only illuminated as far as her throat, leaving her face in darkness; she looked as if she were sleeping, but when the tip of the brush grazed her skin her tremulous quivering told him that she was wide awake. Her calm acceptance of all these things made her seem to him something sacred. Whether human, animal or plant, she could not be called a "person," but then she wasn't exactly some feral creature either—more like a mysterious being with qualities of both.

When he eventually set the brush down, he looked down at her body, at the flowers blooming on it, with all thoughts of filming gone out of his head. But the sunlight was gradually failing, her face being slowly erased by the late-afternoon shadows, and so he quickly set his thoughts in order and stood up.

"Lie on your side for me." Slowly, as though timing her

movements to some music only she could hear, she bent her arms, legs and waist and rolled onto her side. He panned the camera down the ridge of her side and over the soft curve of her buttocks, then filmed first the flowers on her back, the flowers of night, and then the flowers of the sun on her front. Once he'd finished this he moved on to her Mongolian mark, faint like some blue relic in the gradually fading light. He hesitated, he'd promised himself he wouldn't do this, but as she gazed over at the pitch-black window he couldn't stop himself from taking a close-up of her face. The screen filled with her pale lips, the shadowed hollow above her protruding collarbones, her forehead with her disheveled hair, and her two empty eyes.

She stood in front of the door with her arms folded while he loaded the equipment into the car trunk. As M had asked, he pushed the key inside one of the hiking boots that had been left on the landing.

"All done," he said. "Let's be off." Even though she was wearing his sweater over her own, she was shivering as though cold. "Shall we go and eat something at yours? Or if you're hungry, how about we find somewhere to eat around here?"

"Whatever you like," she murmured, then gestured toward her chest. "Will this come off with water?" As though this practical detail was the only thing she was curious about.

"I wouldn't have thought it'd come off too easily. You'll have to wash it a few times to—" She interrupted him.

"I don't want it to come off."

Momentarily at a loss, he looked across at her face, but the darkness obscured whatever expression might have been there.

* * *

Heading into a more built-up area, they tried a few different alleys in their search for somewhere to eat. As she didn't eat meat, they chose a place that advertised Buddhist cuisine. They ordered the set meal, and around twenty neatly arranged side dishes were brought out, alongside stone-pot rice with chestnuts and ginseng. Watching her as she ate, it suddenly occurred to him that, despite her having spent the past four hours stark naked, nothing he'd done had drawn from her any meaningful response. Of course, his plan hadn't been to get her aroused, only to film her naked, but all the same it was surprising that the process hadn't provoked in her even the slightest feelings of desire.

Now, as she sat across from him wearing his chunky sweater and with her spoon in her mouth, he felt that the miracle of that afternoon, which had finally succeeded in neutralizing the persistent, agonizing desire of the past year, was well and truly over. The imagined sight of him throwing her down, rough enough to make all the people in the restaurant scream if they could see it, descended in front of her moving lips like a semi-transparent veil, an all-too-familiar hellish projection flickering in front of his eyes. He looked down at the table and awkwardly swallowed a mouthful of rice.

"Why is it you don't eat meat? I've always wondered, but somehow I couldn't ask." She lowered her chopsticks and looked across at him. "You don't have to tell me if it's difficult for you," he said, fighting all the time to suppress the sexual images that were running through his head.

"No," she said calmly. "It isn't difficult. It's just that I don't think you'd understand." She raised her chopsticks again and slowly chewed some seasoned bean sprouts. "It's because of a dream I had."

"A dream?" he repeated.

"I had a dream . . . and that's why I don't eat meat."

"Well . . . what kind of dream?"

"I dreamed of a face."

"A face?"

Seeing how utterly baffled he was, she laughed quietly. A melancholic laugh. "Didn't I say you wouldn't understand?"

He couldn't ask: in that case, why did you use to bare your breasts to the sunlight, like some kind of mutant animal that had evolved to be able to photosynthesize? Was that because of a dream too?

He parked the car in front of her building, and they both got out.

"Thank you so much for today."

She smiled in response. Her smile was quiet and thoughtful, not dissimilar to that of his wife. For all the world as though she were a perfectly ordinary woman. It's true, he thought, she really is ordinary. It's me who's the crazy one.

She went in through the main door to the building, vanishing without bowing good-bye. He stood there and waited for the lights to come on in her room, then, when her window still hadn't lit up, got back in the car and started the engine. In his mind he sketched her darkened room, and her sliding her naked body, still covered with the brilliant flowers, between the mattress and the quilt. That body which he had spent so many hours close beside, yet which he had touched only with the tip of his brush.

He ached.

* * *

When he pressed the buzzer for 709 it was exactly twenty minutes past nine. The woman who opened the door and came out said in a hushed voice, "Ji-woo's been asking for his mother; he's just fallen asleep a few minutes ago." A little girl—judging by her braids, she was in the second or third year of primary school—held out Ji-woo's plastic forklift truck for him to take. He thanked them and put the truck in his backpack. He left the door to his apartment, 710, open, and carried the sleeping child through carefully. The walk down the corridor to the child's bedroom felt unusually long. Ji-woo couldn't have been sleeping very deeply, because as soon as he laid him down in the bed he could hear the wet sound of the boy sucking his thumb, a lonely sound in the darkened room.

He went into the living room and turned on the light, locked the front door and sat down on the sofa. He remained lost in thought for a while, then stood up, went back over to the door, opened it and went out. After taking the lift down to the ground floor, he went and sat in the driver's seat of the parked car. While he was busy rummaging around in the bag that held the two 6mm tapes and the sketchbook, his phone rang.

"Ji-woo?" His wife's voice sounded subdued.

"He's asleep."

"Did he have dinner?"

"He must have done. He was already asleep when I got there."

"Okay. I'll be back around eleven."

"He's sleeping so deeply I . . . well."

"What?"

"I'm just going to pop to the studio. There's something I haven't quite finished yet." His wife didn't answer. "I'm sure Ji-woo won't wake up. He's really sound asleep. You know he sleeps through till morning these days." Nothing.

"Are you listening?" Still nothing.

"Darling."

To his surprise, it sounded as though she were crying. Was there no one else in the shop? It would be highly unusual for her to let herself cry in front of others, she who was always so acutely aware of prying eyes.

After a while she appeared to have calmed herself down, and spoke in a voice he'd never heard from her before, such was the complex mix of emotions it seemed to express: "If you want to go, then go. I'm going to close up the shop and head home now."

She hung up. Ordinarily, she was the kind of person who could never bring herself to hang up first, no matter how busy she was. Thrown into confusion, he felt an unexpected pang of guilt and sat there for a while undecided, still clutching the phone in his hand. He hesitated over whether to go back inside and wait for his wife to get in, but soon made up his mind and started the engine. The roads were fairly empty at this hour; it would only take her twenty minutes or so to get home. In all likelihood, the child would stay sound asleep and nothing at all would happen. But in any case, he simply couldn't face the thought of sitting there in that brightly lit apartment, waiting for his wife to come home, only to be confronted with the darkness in her face.

When he arrived at the studio there was only J there.

"You're here late! I was just about to leave."

He hoped that J wouldn't hang around on his account. Given that the space was shared by four people, and all of them night owls, the opportunity for a whole night's uninterrupted work was rare.

He turned on the computer while J was getting his things together and putting on his trench coat. J seemed surprised to see the two tapes he was holding.

"You've made something."

"That's right."

J smiled at his lack of elaboration. "I'd love to take a look at it when you're done."

"Of course."

J sketched a playful bow, opened the door and swung his arms vigorously as he marched out, impersonating someone who felt the need to make himself scarce. He laughed. Once the laughter had subsided, it struck him what a long time it had been since he'd laughed like that.

The sun was well up the next day when he took out the master tape and turned off the computer.

The tapes had turned out better than he'd expected. The lighting, her movements, the atmosphere these evoked—all were breathtakingly compelling. He toyed briefly with the idea of adding some background music, before deciding to keep it silent, to make it seem as though everything on-screen were occurring in a kind of vacuum. Her gentle tossing, her naked body littered with gorgeous blooms, the Mongolian mark—against a background of silence, a soundless harmony recalling something primeval, something eternal.

He struggled through the tedious process of rendering for

what felt like an age, smoking his way through an entire pack of cigarettes, sticking at it until it was done. The running time of the finished piece was four minutes fifty-five seconds. It began with a shot of his hand as he painted her prone body, faded out on the Mongolian mark, and then, after a shot capturing the desert of her face, her features so shadowed she was almost unrecognizable, faded out again.

It was a long time since he'd known the exhaustion that comes from staying up all night. He felt as if grains of sand were embedded here and there in his skin, a sense of everything having taken on some alien form. He wrote on the label of the master tape with a black pen: "Mongolian Mark 1—Flowers of Night and Flowers of Day."

As soon as he was finished he put his hands over his eyes, consumed by the thought of that image that he knew he should never attempt to capture, but to which, were such a thing possible, he would affix the title "Mongolian Mark 2."

The image of a man and woman, their bodies made brilliant with painted flowers, having sex against a background of unutterable silence. Their shifting limbs matter-of-fact in that vacuum. A progression of scenes lurching from violence to tenderness, with no extreme left unexplored. One stripped-down, drawn-out moment of quiet purification, extremity sublimated into some kind of peace.

He clutched the master tape, running his fingers over it while the thoughts ran through his head. If he was to choose a man to be filmed having sex with his sister-in-law, whoever it was it couldn't be him. He was all too aware of his wrinkled stomach, his love handles, his sagging buttocks and thighs.

He started the car, but instead of driving home he headed to a nearby sauna. He changed into the white T-shirt and shorts they gave him at the desk, and gazed, disillusioned, at his reflection in the mirror. There was no doubt about it: it couldn't be him. But then who? Whom could he find to have sex with her? He wasn't making a porn movie, nor was it enough for them to just feign the motions. He needed authenticity, and that meant actual penetration. But then who? Who would agree to such a thing? And how would his sister-in-law react?

He knew he had reached a point of no return. But he couldn't stop now. No, he didn't want to stop.

He tried to fall asleep in the sauna, his dangling limbs caressed by the warm steam. The place felt like being inside a summer night, time doubling back on itself. Enveloped by the warm radiance of that image, the only image that was forbidden him, all the energy drained from his exhausted body.

The first thing he saw when he woke from his brief sleep was her.

Her skin was a pale green. Her body lay prone in front of him, like a leaf that had just fallen from the branch, only barely begun to wither. The Mongolian mark was gone; instead, her whole body was covered evenly with that pale wash of green.

He turned her over onto her back. A dazzling light came from her naked body, making him squint, and he couldn't see the area above her breasts—as though the source of the light was somewhere around her face. He spread her legs; her thighs parted with an ease that could only mean she was awake. A green sap, like that which oozes from bruised leaves, began to flow out from her vagina when he entered her. The acrid sweetness of the grass was so pungent he found it difficult to breathe. When he pulled out, on the point of climax, he saw that the whole of his penis was stained green. A blackish paste was smeared over his skin from his lower stomach to his thighs, a fresh sap which could have come from either her or him.

Once again he was on the phone to her, confronting silence on the other end of the line.

"Sister-in-law . . ."

"Yes." Luckily, this time she answered without too long a pause. Did she sound like she was glad to hear from him? He wasn't sure.

"Did you get a good rest yesterday?"

"Yes."

"So, there's something I wanted to ask you."

"Go ahead."

"Have you washed the flowers off?"

"No."

He exhaled in a long sigh. "In that case, can you keep it on for now? Just until tomorrow. It won't have faded by then. I, uh, I have to film you one more time."

Was she laughing? He wished he could see her expression. Was she smiling?

"I didn't want it to come off," she said calmly, "so I haven't washed my body. It's stopping the dreams from coming. If it comes off later I hope you'll paint it on again for me."

He couldn't understand exactly what she was saying, but he gripped the receiver tightly, and muttered, good. Perhaps she would agree after all. Perhaps she would agree to what he had in mind.

"If you have time, could you come around again tomorrow? To the studio at Sonbawi."

"Okay."

"And there'll be someone else coming too. A man." She was silent. "I'm going to have him take his clothes off and paint flowers on him too. That's okay, right?" He waited. Her long silences no longer made him uneasy; he thought he'd figured out by now that they generally signified consent.

"Okay."

He put the phone down and paced around and around the living room, wringing his hands.

He called his wife. It would be unpleasant, but it had to be done.

"Where are you?" she asked, her tone more ambivalent than cold.

"At home."

"How did your work go?"

"It's still going. It looks like I'll be busy until tomorrow night."

"I see. Well . . . don't work too hard."

He hung up. He would have preferred it if she'd screamed and raged like other wives, nagged and heaped abuse on him. She became resigned so easily, and her habit of gloomily suppressing the dregs of this resignation suffocated him. He didn't know if her desperate efforts to be understanding and considerate were a good or a bad thing. Perhaps it was all down to him being self-centered and irresponsible. But right now he found his wife's patience and desire to do the right thing stifling, which made him still more inclined to see it as a flaw in her character.

Once the vague mix of guilt, regret and uncertainty had passed, he continued with the next stage of his plan and dialed J's number.

"J? Will you be coming by this evening?"

"No, I was there all last night. I'm going to take a break today."

"Ah, really? I have to ask you a small favor."

"What sort of favor?"

"Are you free tomorrow? I'm going to be doing some filming tomorrow evening." He told J the location of M's studio. He was about to add that it was fine if J was only free in the afternoon, that it wouldn't take long, but then he changed his mind. "You said you wanted to see the work I made yesterday, right?"

"Of course."

"Well, I'm heading over to the studio now." He hung up.

J was early. Though he was usually so laid-back, today, for the first time, he seemed impatient.

"I'm shaking."

He made J a cup of coffee and mentally stripped him. Good: the two of them would suit each other.

The previous afternoon, when he'd shown J the tape, the younger man had been incredibly excited.

"I can't believe it . . . it's magical! I mean, how did this sort of idea come to you in the first place? You know, for a while I actually thought you were a pretty average guy . . . ah, I'm sorry . . ." J's voice, the look in his eyes, were filled with an almost suspiciously excessive enthusiasm. Was he being sincere? "This is so different from anything you've made before. This is . . . it's like something's lifted you right up to a completely different level! These colors!"

Though he balked at J's hyperbole—typical of young people—overall he had to say he agreed. It wasn't as though he'd previously been blind to the beauty of color, but still. It felt as though his body were brimming with their intense hues, all this latent energy inside him—it was almost unbearable. He was living with a new intensity.

"I used to be dark": There were times when he wanted to express it this way. I used to be dark. I was in a dark place. The monochrome world, entirely devoid of the colors he was now experiencing, had had a calmness that was beautiful in its way, but it wasn't somewhere he could go back to. It seemed the happiness that had enabled him to feel that quiet peace was now lost to him forever. And yet he found himself unable to think of this as a loss. All of his energy was taken up in trying to cope with the excitement, the heightened awareness of living in the present moment.

Encouraged by J's praise, though he couldn't prevent his face from flushing, he eventually managed to get out the words he'd planned. But when he showed him his sketchbook and the dance performance program and asked him if he would do him the favor of modeling for him, J became flustered.

"Why on earth are you asking me? There are plenty of professional models out there; you could hire a theater actor, or . . ."

"You've got the right kind of body. Anything too gym honed would be all wrong. You're just the thing."

"No, I'm not the one for this job—to pose like that with this woman. I can't."

"No one will know. I won't show your face. And this woman, don't you want to meet her? Wouldn't you like to be part of the inspiration for such a piece?"

After being given just the one night to think it over, J had called the next morning and agreed to be the model. Of course, there was no way the younger man could guess what he really wanted: to film the two of them, J and his sister-in-law, actually having sex.

"She's a bit late, isn't she?" J asked, peering nervously out of the window. He'd already been growing impatient himself. She'd assured him that she'd be able to find the place on her own, so he'd decided to wait for her at the studio rather than meeting at the underground station.

"Well, perhaps I'll go down to the station." He picked up his sweater and stood up, but just then they heard someone knocking on the translucent glass door. "Ah, here she is!"

J put down his cup of coffee.

This time she was wearing a chunky black sweater, with the same jeans as before. Her loose hair, naturally very black, was still wet; she must have washed it just before she came out. She looked first at him, then at J, then gave a quick laugh.

"I was very careful," she said, touching her hair. "I didn't get any water on the flowers."

J smiled, looking relieved. He probably hadn't expected her to seem so ordinary.

"Take off your clothes."

"Me?" J's eyes opened wide.

"She's already been painted, so now I just have to do you." Stifling a nervous giggle, J turned his back on them and got undressed. "You'll have to take your pants off, too." J hesitated, then did as he was asked. J's body was slight, more so than he'd expected. Aside from the thick hair that ran down in a line from his belly button and spread to the tops of his thighs, his flesh was enviably white and smooth.

Just as he'd done with his sister-in-law, he had J lie prone and began to paint him with flowers, starting from the nape of his neck. Working as quickly as possible, he used a big brush to paint light purple hydrangeas, which seemed to tumble down over J's back as though caught in a strong wind.

"Turn over."

Using J's penis as the center, he painted a single huge flower, the crimson of blood, so that it looked as though J's black pubic hair was the sepals, and his penis the pistil. She sat quietly on the sofa all the while, sipping a cup of tea and carefully watching him work. When he was done, he noticed that J's penis had stiffened slightly.

After painting the rest of the flowers on J's torso he took a quick breather, then stood up and replaced the tape in the camcorder with a new one, wanting to make sure there would be plenty of running time. He turned to her and asked her to take her clothes off.

She did as he asked. The light wasn't as strong as it had been the last time, but the golden cluster of flowers that he'd painted right in the center of her chest still sparkled brilliantly. In contrast to J, she was perfectly composed, as if declaring how much more natural it was to not wear clothes. When she knelt down on the sheet, the entranced look on J's face didn't escape him.

Without his giving her any directions, she moved closer to J, and he, as though mirroring her, got into a kneeling position. There was something desolate in the contrast between her still, silent face and her radiant body.

"What should we do now?" J asked, his face red. He was probably nervous at the prospect of having to take the lead; all the same, his penis had stiffened again.

"Sit her on your knees." He thought it best to refer to her as simply "her." Now he picked up the camcorder and approached them. "Pull her close. Damn it, haven't you ever done this before? You're supposed to be acting. Try touching her breasts or something."

J wiped his forehead with the back of his hand. But before he could do anything she slowly maneuvered around to face and then straddle him. She slid her hand behind J's neck and drew him toward her, while her other hand began to stroke the red flower on his chest. Marked with nothing but the breathing of the three people, an amount of time passed that would be impossible to measure. J's nipples quietly hardened and his penis became erect. She rubbed her neck against J's like they were two birds caressing, almost as if she'd seen his sketches and knew exactly what he wanted her to do.

"Good. Really good." He filmed the scene from several angles, eventually finding the best one. "Good . . . keep going. Lie down like that, on top of each other."

She put her hand on J's chest and gently pushed him down onto the sheet, then reached out and began to stroke the red flowers that led down over J's torso, taking them one by one and slowly making her way toward his crotch. He moved behind her with the camcorder, making sure to capture the dark purple flowers scattered over her back, the Mongolian mark rippling in time with her movements. He clenched his teeth and thought to himself, this is it. Now if only it could be even better.

J's penis was already fully erect, and he was grimacing as though he couldn't bear the pressure any longer. She slowly lay down on her stomach, her breasts resting on J's chest and her buttocks lifting up into the space above them. He filmed the two of them side-on. There was something obscene about the way her back was arched like a cat's, about the unpainted space around

J's belly button, about his rigid penis. They were almost like two huge, abstracted plants. When she slowly sat up straight, straddling J's hips, he stammered:

"Perhaps . . . I mean, I was just thinking." He looked at her and J in turn. "Could you maybe do it, you know, for real?"

There was no flicker of shock or revulsion in her face, but J suddenly pushed her away as though her skin were burning him. He got to his knees, awkwardly trying to conceal his penis.

"What? You want to make some kind of a porno?"

"If you don't feel like it, that's fine. But if it were possible for you to just naturally . . ."

"That's it, I'm done." J stood up.

"Just a minute, wait. I won't ask you to do anything more. Just what you've been doing so far." He grabbed J by the shoulder. Perhaps he'd used more force than he'd intended, because J grunted and pushed his hand away.

"Hey, come on . . . there's no need for that."

A silent pause. J seemed to soften a little.

"I understand . . . I'm an artist too, after all. But this kind of thing just . . . no. Who is this woman, anyway? She doesn't seem like a prostitute. And even if she were, it still wouldn't be okay, you know?"

"I understand. Really, I do. I'm sorry."

J got back onto the sheet, but the sexually charged atmosphere of a few minutes ago had completely fizzled out. He put his arms around her and laid her down, his face set hard as though this were all some form of punishment. Their bodies overlapped like two petals, and she closed her eyes. If J had agreed, she would have gone along without a murmur of protest. He felt sure of that.

"Try moving a bit."

Slowly, J moved his body back and forth in a pained, stilted mimicry of sex. He watched as the soles of her feet curled up and her hands clasped J's waist. Her body was sufficiently animated, flushed with desire, to make up for J's passivity. They spent ten minutes or so in that position, every second of which was clearly repulsive to J, though to him it felt all too short. Still, he managed to get the angles he'd wanted, and some decent images for the tape.

"Are we all done now?" J asked. His skin was flushed red right up to his hair, but it wasn't from arousal.

"Just once more . . . this is the last time." He swallowed. "From behind. Make her lie on her stomach. This really is the last time. It's the most important scene. Don't say you can't." J burst into a laughter that sounded more like sobbing.

"That's it. That's really it. I'm going to stop now before this gets any worse. You've got plenty of inspiration. Now I know what it feels like for porno actors. It's miserable!"

He put a restraining hand on J's shoulder, but J shook him off and began to get dressed. He gritted his teeth and watched as his work, the still-intact whirl of flowers, disappeared beneath J's plain-colored shirt. "It's not that I don't understand, okay? Don't think I'm some kind of prude. I guess I'm just more . . . more restrained than I thought I was. I agreed to do it because I was curious, but I just can't go through with it. I guess there are just parts of myself that I need to, to awaken, but . . . I need some time first, I'm sorry."

J was evidently sincere, and seemed hurt more than anything else. The young man bowed to him, giving only a cursory glance over in her direction, then walked briskly to the door.

* * *

"I'm sorry," he said as J's car roared out of the front yard. She didn't reply, just put on her sweater and stepped into her jeans. But then, instead of zipping them up, she just giggled into the air.

"Why are you laughing?"

"Because I'm all wet . . ."

He looked over at her, feeling as dazed as though he'd just received a blow to the head. She had her hand on the half-up zipper and was hesitating, looking as though she couldn't bring herself to pull it either up or down. Only then did he realize that he was still holding the camcorder. He set it down, strode over to the door, which J had left open, and locked it. Just in case, he put the upper security chain on too. Walking over almost at a run, he clutched her to him and the two of them tumbled down onto the sheet. When he tugged her jeans down to her knees she said, "No."

It wasn't just verbally that she rejected him—she shoved him away roughly, stood up and pulled her jeans back up. He watched as she did up the zipper and fastened the button. He stood up, stepped close to her and pushed her still-fevered body up against the wall. But when he pressed his lips firmly against hers, probing with his tongue, she shoved him away again.

"Why shouldn't we? Because I'm your brother-in-law?"

"No, it's nothing to do with that."

"Then why not? Come on, you said you were all wet!" She was silent. "Did you fancy that kid?"

"It wasn't him, it was the flowers . . ."

"The flowers?"

Her face instantly blanched, as if in fear. Her lower lip, red and swollen from worrying it with her teeth, trembled imperceptibly.

"I really wanted to do it," she said carefully. "I've never wanted it so much before. It was the flowers on his body . . . I couldn't help myself. That's all."

He watched as she turned her back on him and walked decisively over to the door. As she scrunched her feet into her trainers he shouted over to her: "If . . ." He couldn't keep a shrill note from his voice. "If I painted flowers on myself, would you do it then?"

She turned around and stared back at him, and he understood her gaze to be one of complicity.

"And . . . I could film it?"

She laughed. Faintly, as if there were nothing she wouldn't do, as if limits and boundaries no longer held any meaning for her. Or else, as if in quiet mockery.

I wish I were dead.

I wish I were dead.

So die.

Unable to understand why the tears were streaming down his face, he clutched the steering wheel and set the wipers to frequent, only to realize that it wasn't the windshield that was blurred but his own vision. He couldn't understand why the words "I wish I were dead" were ceaselessly being hammered out inside his head like an incantation. Nor could he understand why the words "so die" would inevitably follow, as though the response were coming from someone inside him, and yet not him. And he couldn't understand how that simple mantra, like a conversation between two strangers, could be sufficient to calm his shuddering body.

He lowered the windows all the way down, on both the driver's side and the passenger's. The car raced along the dark highway amid the roar of the wind and the nighttime traffic. The trembling started in his hands and then spread through his whole body, so he gritted his teeth and pressed down on the accelerator. Every time he glanced at the speedometer he was shocked by how fast he was going, and rubbed his eyes with shaking fingers.

Wearing a white cardigan over a black dress, P walked up to the main gate of the apartment building. The two of them had dated for four years, until she broke up with him. Later, she'd married one of her primary school classmates, who'd passed the bar examinations. Her husband was the main breadwinner, but she'd managed to successfully combine married life with her own work. She'd held several private exhibitions, becoming something of a name among the Gangnam collectors, which had of course provoked a flurry of jealous slander from those who knew her.

P soon noticed the car, as he'd left the front and back emergency lights on. He drove down toward the gate and shouted, "Get in!"

"Anyone might recognize me here—hell, even the porter knows my face. What on earth do you want at this time of night?"

"Just get in. I've something to tell you." P reluctantly did as he asked. "It's been a while, I know. Sorry for calling you up out of the blue like that."

"You're right, it *has* been a while. And this isn't like you. I don't believe you just had a sudden urge to see me again."

He rubbed his forehead impatiently. "I have a favor to ask."

"Go on."

"It's a long story. Let's go to your studio. Is it nearby?"

"Just a five-minute walk . . . but won't you tell me what's going on?" P shouted at him, her strident tone demanding that he hurry up and give her a straight answer. She'd always been hot tempered. He was suddenly glad of her vitality, of her strong character, which he had at one time found somewhat wearying. A sudden impulse to embrace her gripped him, then faded away as abruptly as it had come. Just the vague memory of an old emotion.

"It's a good thing my husband's working tonight," said P, switching on the studio lights. "Otherwise there might've been one hell of a misunderstanding."

"Take a look at the sketches I mentioned." He held them out to her and she gave them her full attention, an earnest expression on her face.

"Interesting. You know, I'm surprised. I didn't know you knew how to use color like this. So." She rubbed her sagging jawline. "This is quite an about-turn. Could you really exhibit something like this? Your nickname used to be 'the May priest,' you know. After Gwangju, your art was so *engagé*, almost as though you were atoning for surviving the May massacre. You seemed so serious, so ascetic . . . all very romantic, I have to admit." P peered at him closely over her glasses. "I can see you're aiming to transform your image, but . . . isn't this a little extreme? Of course, it isn't for me to argue the pros and cons."

Not wanting to get into a debate with P, he kept quiet and began to take off his clothes.

P seemed a little surprised but nevertheless resigned as she mixed the paints in the palette and selected a brush. "Well," she murmured, "it's certainly been a long time since I last saw you naked."

Slowly, painstakingly, P began to paint. The brush was cold, and the sensation was ticklish yet numbing, a persistent, effectual caress.

"I'll make sure my personal style doesn't come through. I mean, I like flowers too, so I've drawn plenty in my time, but yours have a distinctive energy about them. I'll bring your drawings to life."

It was well past midnight when P finally announced that she was finished.

"Thanks," he said, shivering from the cold.

"If there was a mirror I'd show it to you."

He looked down at his chest, stomach and legs, all covered with goose pimples, and at the huge red flowers painted there.

"I like it. You're better at it than me."

"I'm not quite sure about how the back's turned out. In your sketches it seemed like you'd put more emphasis on the back."

"I'm sure it's great. Given your reputation, that is."

"I tried to paint them the way you drew them, not how I'd choose to do it myself, but I guess I couldn't stop a little bit of myself coming through."

"I'm really grateful."

Only then did P laugh. "Actually, when you took your clothes off I got kind of turned on . . ."

"Oh?" he remarked absentmindedly, hurriedly slipping his clothes on. He felt a little warmer with his sweater on, but his limbs were still stiff.

"Now, for some reason . . ."

"What?"

"It looks wrong. Seeing you with your whole body covered in flowers, it feels kind of . . . pitiful. I never felt that way about you before . . ." P came over and finished buttoning up his shirt for him. "I should at least get a kiss, seeing as you called me up in the middle of the night."

Before he'd had the chance to respond, P pressed her lips to his. The kiss was a palimpsest of memories, of all the countless kisses they'd shared in the past. He felt as though he were about to cry, but he couldn't tell whether it was because of happy memories, or friendship, or fear of the boundary he was intending soon to cross.

It was late, so he knocked softly on the door rather than press the buzzer. Instead of waiting for an answer, he tried the handle. As he'd expected, the door opened.

He stepped into the pitch-black living room. The glass door to the veranda let in the pale gleam from the streetlights, but it wasn't bright enough for him to be able to make out anything. His foot bumped against the shoe cupboard.

"Are you asleep?"

He set the filming equipment down by the front door; it was heavy, and he'd had to carry some of it slung over his shoulders as well as what he could carry in his hands. When he took off his shoes and moved over in the direction of the mattress, he could make out the faint outline of a person sitting there. Even in the darkness, he could still tell that she was naked. She got up and came toward him.

"Shall I turn on the light?" His voice was hoarse with desire.

"You smell . . . ," she said in a low voice, ". . . of paint."

He groaned and reached out for her, forgetting about the lighting, the camcorder, everything. None of that existed now.

He laid her down with a snarl, clutching at her breasts with one hand and haphazardly sucking her lips and nose as he hurriedly unbuttoned his shirt. He tugged at the lower buttons, tearing them off in his haste.

As soon as he was naked he pushed her legs wide apart and entered her. A constant panting sound, as if from a wild animal, was coming from somewhere, interspersed with a moaning that rose into an eerie shriek. When he realized that these noises were coming from him, he shuddered; he'd never made a sound during sex, had always thought of it as the preserve of flirtatious young women. Into her already soaking wet vagina, which was contracting alarmingly, he released a jet of semen with a gasp of pain, falling forward as though swooning.

"I'm sorry," he said, reaching out for her face in the darkness.

"Can I turn on the light?" she asked. She sounded perfectly composed.

"What for?"

"I want to be able to see you properly." She stood up and walked over to the switch. Their sex had been fairly one-sided, and hadn't even lasted five minutes, so it was no wonder she didn't seem tired.

When she flicked the lights on he shaded his eyes from the sudden glare. He waited, blinking, until he was able to lower his hands. She was leaning against the wall. The flowers scattered over her body were as beautiful as ever.

Suddenly self-conscious, he put his hands over his paunch and tried to suck it in.

"Don't cover it . . . I like it. The petals look like they're wrinkled."

She slowly came toward him. She bent over and, as she'd done with J, reached out and began to stroke the flowers on his chest.

"Just a minute." Still naked, he stood up and went over to the front door, where he'd left the equipment. He set the tripod up, quite low, and fixed the camcorder in place, then pushed the mattress out onto the veranda, and spread the white sheet, which he'd brought with him, out on the floor. He set up the lighting just as it had been in M's studio.

"Can you lie down?"

Once she was lying down he estimated where their entwined bodies would end up, and adjusted the camcorder accordingly.

She lay stretched out under the blinding spotlight. He carefully lowered himself on top of her. Would their bodies look like overlapping petals, as they had with her and J? Would they seem like one body, a hybrid of plant, animal and human?

Every time they changed position he readjusted the camcorder. Before he took her from behind, which J had refused to do, he first took a long close-up of her buttocks. After he inserted himself, he checked how the image looked in the exterior monitor, then started to thrust.

Everything was perfect. It was just like in his sketches. His red flower closed and opened repeatedly above her Mongolian mark, his penis slipping in and out of her like a huge pistil. He shuddered at the appalling nature of their union, a union of images that were somehow repellent and yet compellingly beautiful. Every time he closed his eyes he could see the lower half of his body dyed green, soaked from the stomach to the thighs with a sticky, grassy sap.

Forever, he gasped, all of this forever, as an unendurable sense of satiation shuddered through his body and she burst into tears. She who hadn't let slip a single moan in close to thirty minutes, whose lips had merely trembled at times, who had kept her eyes closed and communicated her keen ecstasy to him purely through the movements of her body. And now it had to end. He raised himself into a sitting position. Still clasping her to him, he moved over to the camcorder, groped for the button and switched it off.

The image he'd wanted to capture on film had to be one that could be repeated over and over, forbidden either to end or to come to a climax. And so, this was where the filming had to stop. He waited until her sobs had subsided before laying her back down on the sheet. In their final minutes of sex she gnashed her teeth, screamed rough and shrill, spat out a panting "stop" and then, at the end, she cried again.

And then everything grew quiet.

In the dark blue light of dawn, he licked her buttocks for a long time.

"I wish I could transfer it onto my tongue."

"What?"

"This Mongolian mark." She turned and looked at him over her shoulder, seeming surprised. "How come you've still got it?"

"I don't know. I used to think everyone had them. But then I went to the public baths one day . . . and I saw that I was the only one."

He held her at the waist and stroked the mark, wishing that he could share it with her, that it could be seared onto his skin like a brand. *I want to swallow you, have you melt into me and flow through my veins.*

"Will the dreams stop now?" she muttered, her voice barely audible.

"Dreams? Ah, the face . . . that's right, you said it was a face, no?" he said, feeling drowsiness slowly creep through his body. "What kind of face? Whose face?"

"It's different every time. Sometimes it feels very familiar, other times I'm sure I've never seen it before. There are times when it's all bloody . . . and times when it looks like the face of a rotting corpse."

He looked her in the eye, his own eyes heavy with the effort of staying open. She, on the other hand, didn't look the least bit tired; her eyes were agitated as she attempted to convey the cause of her affliction. "I thought it was all because of eating meat," she said. "I thought all I had to do was to stop eating meat and then the faces wouldn't come back. But it didn't work." He knew he ought to concentrate on what she was saying, but he couldn't stop his eyes from gradually falling closed. "And so . . . now I know. The face is inside my stomach. It rose up from inside my stomach." With her words sounding in his ears like a lullaby, one he could make neither head nor tail of, he plunged over the edge of consciousness and into a seemingly bottomless sleep. "But I'm not scared anymore. There's nothing to be scared of now."

When he woke up she was still sleeping.

The sunlight coming into the room was bright. Her disheveled hair wrapped her head like an animal's mane, while the crumpled sheet was coiled around her lower body. The smell of her body filled the room, a sour, tangy smell with notes of sweetness, bitterness, and a rank animal musk.

What time was it? He fished his mobile out of the pocket of his sweater, which he'd hurriedly tossed aside the previous night.

One in the afternoon. He'd fallen asleep sometime around six a.m., which meant he'd been sleeping like the dead for seven straight hours. He pulled on his pants and trousers and looked around for his equipment. He packed up the tripod and lighting, but he couldn't see the camcorder anywhere. He remembered putting it down after he'd finished filming, right by the front door so it wouldn't get knocked over; but now it was nowhere to be seen.

Could she have briefly woken up earlier and put it away somewhere? He went to take a look in the kitchen. Heading toward the sink behind the partition, he noticed something shiny that had fallen to the floor. It was the 6mm tape. Strange, he thought, then rubbed his eyes and took a proper look around him. There was a woman sitting with her face resting on the table. His wife.

There was a wrapped lunch box next to her elbow, and her limp fingers clutched her mobile. The camcorder was upside down underneath the table, its deck open. She must have heard him as he moved toward her, but she didn't stir.

"D . . . darling," he said. His head was swimming; he couldn't believe this was happening. Only then did she lift her head from the table and stand up, but he quickly realized that she wasn't planning to come anywhere near him. Instead, she seemed to want to keep the table between them, to stop him from getting too close.

"I hadn't heard anything from Yeong-hye, so . . . so I thought I'd stop by on my way to the shop. I just happened to have made some seasoned vegetables, you see." Her voice was incredibly tense. She was struggling to maintain her composure, as though she were the one trying to justify herself. He knew that tone. It was the slow, low, faintly tremulous tone that meant she was fighting to conceal extreme emotion.

"The door was open, so I came in. Then I saw that Yeong-hye was all covered in paint, and I thought, that's strange . . . I didn't recognize you at first, because your face was turned to the wall and your body was covered by the quilt." Still clutching her mobile, she brushed her hair back from her face. Both her hands were shaking visibly. "I guessed Yeong-hye had found a man, or maybe that she'd gone crazy for the second time, what with that stuff on her body . . . I knew I ought to just get out of there, but . . . that man could have been anyone, and what if Yeong-hye needed my protection . . . then I spotted the camcorder by the door, and I picked it up and rewound the tape, just like you taught me, ages ago . . ." She was having to exercise extreme self-control, squeezing out every ounce of her courage so that she could go on. "And I saw you on the tape."

In her eyes there was a mixture of shock, fear and despair that couldn't be expressed in words, whereas her facial expression looked almost callous. Only then did he realize that his naked body seemed to be actively disgusting her, and he hurriedly looked about for his shirt.

He found it by the bathroom, tossed in a crumpled heap, and put it on. "Darling. I can explain. It won't be easy for you to understand, but . . ."

She cut him off abruptly, raising her voice. "I've called the emergency services."

"*What?*" He took a step toward her, incomprehension furrowing his brow.

She backed away. "You and Yeong-hye are both clearly in need of medical treatment."

Several seconds passed before he grasped that she was in earnest. "What are you saying? That you're committing me to a mental hospital?"

Just then a rustling sound came from over by the mattress. Both he and his wife held their breath. Yeong-hye pushed the sheet aside and stood up, stark naked. He saw that tears were streaming from his wife's eyes.

"Bastard," she muttered, swallowing her sobs. "Just look at her . . . she clearly isn't well. In her mind. How could you?"

Up until then, Yeong-hye had seemed oblivious to her sister's presence in the apartment; only now did she look over at the two of them, her face a perfect blank. Her gaze was utterly devoid of any form of expression.

She slowly turned her back on them and walked out onto the veranda. The chill air rushed into the apartment when she opened the sliding door. He fixed his eyes on the pale blue of her Mongolian mark, seeing the traces of his saliva and semen that had dried there like sap. Suddenly it felt to him that he had grown old, had experienced everything there was to experience, and that not even death held any fear for him anymore.

She thrust her glittering golden breasts over the veranda railing. Her legs were covered with scattered orange petals, and she spread them wide as though she wanted to make love to the sunlight, to the wind. He heard the sounds of the approaching ambulance siren, of screams, sighs, the yells of children, all the commotion of the alleyway down below. The sound of feet hurrying up the stairs, coming closer.

He had to rush out onto the veranda, now, and throw himself over the railing against which she was leaning. He would fall down three floors and smash his head to pieces. It was the only way. The only way to make a clean end of all this. And yet he kept on standing there as if rooted to the spot, as if this were the final moment of his life, staring fixedly at the blazing flower that was her body, that body which now glittered with images so much more intense than those he had filmed during the night.

3

Flaming Trees

She stands and looks out at the rain-swept road. She is at the bus stop across from Maseok terminal. Huge goods vans thunder past, speeding along in the fast lane. The raindrops drum against her umbrella, so forcefully it seems they might rip through the material.

She isn't really young anymore, and it would be difficult to call her a beauty, exactly. The curve of her neck is quite attractive and the look in her eyes is open and friendly. She wears light, natural-looking makeup, and her white blouse is neat, uncreased. Thanks to that smart impression, which one might reasonably expect to attract curiosity, attention is deflected away from the faint shadows clouding her face.

Her eyes glimmer briefly; the bus she has been waiting for has appeared in the distance. She steps down into the road. She watches as the bus, which had been tearing along at a great pace, slows down.

"You're going to Ch'ukseong Psychiatric Hospital, right?"

The bus driver, in late middle age, nods to her and motions her up. She pays the fare, and as she scans the bus for somewhere to sit her eyes pass over the faces of the other passengers. They are all watching her closely. Is she a patient, or is she a nurse? There doesn't seem to be anything odd about her. Well used to this, she keeps her eyes averted from those probing gazes, that mix of suspicion, caution, repugnance and curiosity.

She shakes the water off her folded umbrella. The floor of the bus is already wet, black and glistening. It wasn't the kind of rain for which an umbrella could provide sufficient shelter, and so her blouse and trousers are half soaked. The bus picks up speed, racing along the wet road. She struggles to keep her balance as she walks down the aisle. Finding a double seat where both spaces are unoccupied, she takes the one next to the window. The windows have steamed up, so she gets a tissue out of her bag and wipes a patch clear. She watches the streaks of rain lashing the window, with the untouched steadiness unique to those accustomed to solitude. As they reach Maseok, the late-June woods begin to unfurl on either side of the road. There is something battened down about the woods in this torrential rain, like a huge animal suppressing a roar. As it turns up the road to Ch'ukseong mountain, the road gradually narrows and becomes winding, bringing the wet body of the woods undulating nearer. The base of that mountain over there—might those be the woods where, three months ago, her sister, Yeong-hye, had been found? One by one, the black spaces between the trees, concealed by the shaking canopy of rain-lashed leaves, pass in front of her eyes. She turns away from the window.

The hospital staff told her that Yeong-hye had gone missing sometime during the hour that was set aside for the patients to take brief, unaccompanied walks—between two and three in the afternoon. This happened only on fixed days, only for non-serious patients, and only when the rain swelling the black clouds overhead seemed likely to stay there. Apparently, when the nurses had checked on the patients at three, they'd been able to confirm that Yeong-hye hadn't come back. It was only then, they said, that the rain had finally begun to spit, just one or two drops at a time. The entire hospital staff were put on emergency. The management and staff hurriedly set up a roadblock on the corner where the buses and taxis went past. When a patient went missing, one possibility was that they had gone down from the mountains and already got as far as Maseok; or the opposite possibility, that they had in fact gone deeper into the mountains.

The rain had gradually grown heavier as the afternoon wore on. This was March, so when darkness fell it did so very swiftly. It was extremely lucky that one of the nurses, who between them had fanned out and searched every inch of the neighboring mountain, did manage to find Yeong-hye; no, in fact it was nothing short of a miracle. That was what the doctor had said. Apparently this nurse had stumbled upon Yeong-hye in an isolated spot deep in the woods covering the mountain slope, standing there stock-still and soaked with rain as if she herself were one of the glistening trees.

When she'd got the call saying Yeong-hye had disappeared, which came around four in the afternoon, she'd been with her son, Ji-woo, who was six years old. The boy had been running a temperature for several days at that point, and she'd taken him to have his lungs X-rayed. He was standing alone in front of the machine, glancing back and forth between her and the doctor, apprehensive.

"Ms. Kim In-hye?"

"Speaking."

"I'm Kim Yeong-hye's nurse."

This was the first time since Yeong-hye had been admitted

that someone from the hospital had contacted her on her mobile. She herself called them only rarely, to check visiting times or occasionally to ask her sister whether everything was okay. In a composed tone of voice designed to conceal the urgency of the situation, the nurse informed her that Yeong-hye was missing.

"We're doing all we can to find her, but if by chance she turns up at your home, you have to call us right away." Before she hung up the nurse asked, "Is there anywhere else she might possibly have gone? Perhaps to your parents?"

"They live out in the countryside . . . I can contact them if you need me to." She flipped the phone closed and put it in her bag, went into the X-ray room and hugged Ji-woo. He'd lost weight over the past few days, and his body felt light and hot in her arms.

"I did really well, Mum." Perhaps it was just because of the fever, but his face seemed flushed with the expectation of praise.

"That's right, he really didn't move a muscle."

After the doctor told her she didn't think it was pneumonia she hugged Ji-woo again, bundled him into a taxi and was driven home in the rain. She hurriedly washed him, gave him rice porridge and medicine, and put him to bed early. There was no room in her thoughts for her missing sister. She hadn't been able to sleep properly for the five days her son had been ill. And that night, if the fever didn't abate, she would have to take him to be admitted to the general hospital. She was packing Ji-woo's clothes and making sure she had his medical insurance certificate, just in case the need did arise, when the phone rang again. This had been sometime around nine in the evening.

"We've found her."

"Thank goodness. I'll come and visit next week as normal." Her thanks were sincere, but subdued by fatigue. Only after she had hung up did it occur to her that the rain she had seen all day must have been pouring down on the mountain where Yeong-hye had been found too. An indiscriminate connection, their existences briefly aligned.

There was no way for her to judge the accuracy of the scene she saw then in her mind's eye but had never seen in reality. She'd held a wet flannel to her snuffling son's forehead all night, slipping occasionally into a sleep that was more like fainting, and saw a tree flickering in the rain like the spirit of some dead person. Black rain, black woods, the pale patient's uniform, soaked through. Wet hair. Black mountain slope. Yeong-hye, an inchoate mass formed of darkness and water, standing tall like a ghost. Eventually the day dawned, and when she placed the palm of her hand on her son's forehead she was relieved by the coolness she felt there. She got up, went out of the bedroom and stared blankly at the bluish half-light leaching in from the living room veranda.

She curled up on the sofa and tried to sleep. She had to get some sleep before Ji-woo woke up, even if it was only an hour.

Look, sister, I'm doing a handstand; leaves are growing out of my body, roots are sprouting out of my hands . . . they delve down into the earth. Endlessly, endlessly . . . yes, I spread my legs because I wanted flowers to bloom from my crotch; I spread them wide . . .

Yeong-hye's voice, which came to her while she was suspended in that halfway state between sleep and wakefulness, was low and warm at first, then innocent like that of a young child, but the last part was mangled, inaudible, a distorted animal sound. Her eyes snapped open in fright, and she was stung by a waking hatred the likes of which she'd never felt before, before being thrown back into sleep. This time she was standing in front of the bathroom mirror. In the reflection, blood was trickling from her left eye. She quickly reached up to wipe the blood away, but somehow her reflection in the mirror didn't move an inch, only stood there, blood running from a staring eye.

She swung herself up at the sound of Ji-woo's coughing and went into the bedroom. Yeong-hye had sat there hunched in a corner of the room, a long time ago, but now she pushed that image from her mind and clasped her son's small hand, lifting it up as if playing a game. "It's okay now," she muttered, but it wasn't clear who these words were intended to comfort; the boy or herself.

The bus pulls over as it turns up the hill. She steps down and opens her umbrella. She is the only passenger alighting here. Without delay, the bus races off down the road.

The narrow road splits here. One road goes up over the hill. You pass through a tunnel, around fifty meters in length. When you emerge, the other side of the small hospital is visible, flanked by mountains on all sides. The rain is still pouring down, its measured cacophony slightly less vicious. She bends down. As she rolls up her trousers to keep them out of the wet, she notices the flaxleaf fleabane that has broken through the asphalt here and there. She adjusts her heavy bag, trying to ease her shoulders, puts up the umbrella and starts walking toward the hospital.

These days she goes every Wednesday to see how her sister is getting on, but before that rainy day when Yeong-hye went missing, once a month had seemed sufficient. She had walked this road carrying all manner of snacks—fruit, rice cakes, fried tofu stuffed with vinegared rice. It was desolate, with no sign of either vehicles or pedestrians. When she spread out the food on the table in the visiting room, Yeong-hye would silently go through the motions of chewing and swallowing, like a child diligently tackling homework. If she tucked Yeong-hye's hair behind her ears, her sister would look up at her and smile quietly. These were the moments when there might have been nothing at all the matter, the moments that never failed to lighten her heart. Might it be okay, after all, for Yeong-hye to live like this indefinitely? Here, where she didn't have to speak if she didn't want to, didn't have to eat meat if the thought repulsed her? Couldn't the two of them get along just fine with these occasional visits?

Yeong-hye was four years younger than her, enough of an age gap for them not to have been in competition with each other growing up. As small children their young cheeks were frequently left throbbing by their heavy-handed father, and Yeong-hye had provoked in In-hye a sense of responsibility that resembled maternal affection, a need to expend all her energy in looking out for this younger sister. She had watched, marveling, as this same sister, once up to her elbows in the dirt and suffering from a recurring heat rash on the backs of her knees, grew up and got married. The one thing that caused her distress was that, as she got older, Yeong-hye became more and more taciturn. She'd always had this side to her, of course, but she had also been perfectly cheerful and sociable when the occasion called for it. Somehow—not suddenly, but over a period of time—she became difficult to read. So difficult that there were times when she seemed like a total stranger.

A day or two after Ji-woo was born, when Yeong-hye came to the hospital to say hello to her first nephew, rather than congratulating her sister she had simply muttered to herself, "I've never seen such a tiny child . . . so this is what they're like when they've just been born?"

There'd been something faintly unsettling about the quiet smile playing around Yeong-hye's mouth. What seemed to be happening was that Yeong-hye was retreating from herself, becoming as distant to herself as she was to her sister. A forlorn face, behind a mask of composure. This was clearly nothing like the melancholy that sometimes afflicted her husband, and yet in certain respects they were both baffling to her in exactly the same way. They were both descending further into silence.

She enters the tunnel. It's darker inside than usual, on account of the weather. She closes her umbrella and walks. She listens to the ringing echoes of her footsteps. A large speckled moth, a type she's never seen before, flutters up off the surface of the wall, into a darkness saturated with damp. She pauses for a while, looks up at its beating wings. But on the pitch-black tunnel ceiling, the moth stays put, as though conscious of being observed.

Her husband liked to film flying things. Birds, butterflies, airplanes, moths, flies. These scenes of flight, which he always seemed to have inserted into a piece despite an apparent lack of connection to the overall subject, had confused her. She was a layperson when it came to art. Once, she'd asked him why he'd included a particular scene, a two-second clip of the black shadow of a bird soaring slowly up into the air, which he'd put after a scene of a ruined bridge and people crying at a funeral.

"Just because" had been his answer. "I just ended up putting it in. I put it in and I thought it looked good."

And then that familiar silence.

Had she ever really understood her husband's true nature, bound up as it was with that seemingly impenetrable silence? She'd thought, at one time, that it might be revealed in his work, in his video art. In fact, before she met him, she hadn't even been aware that such a field of art existed. Despite her best efforts, though, his works proved incomprehensible to her. Nothing was revealed.

She remembers the late afternoon when they first met. He'd come into her shop, skinny as a sorghum stalk and with several days' worth of stubble on his face, a camcorder bag slung over one shoulder that was clearly weighing him down. He searched out some shaving lotion, brought it to the counter and rested both arms on the glass, looking utterly worn out. He looked like he might collapse, and take the counter with him. It was faintly miraculous the way she, having had practically no romantic experiences up until then, came out with a friendly "Have you had lunch?" As if surprised, but lacking the energy required to express that surprise, he had merely fixed her face with his exhausted gaze. Something in his defenseless state had drawn her to him.

What she'd wanted, from that afternoon, had been to use her own strength to allow him to rest. But despite devoting herself wholeheartedly to this goal, even after they were married he still looked perpetually worn out. He was always busy with his own things, and during what little time he did spend at home he looked more like a traveler putting up there for a night than a man in his own home. His silence had the heavy mass of rock and the tenacious resistance of rubber, particularly when his art wasn't going well.

It wasn't long before she realized something: perhaps the one she'd so earnestly wanted to help was not him but herself. Was it not perhaps her own image—she who had left home at nineteen and gone on to make a life for herself in Seoul, always entirely under her own steam—that she had seen mirrored in this man's exhaustion?

Just as she could not be certain of the source of her affection for him, or if he was really its true object, she had never been entirely sure of his feelings for her. He often seemed to rely on her, being the type for whom daily life was a constant struggle, full of potential pitfalls. He was honest to the point of seeming naive; exaggeration or flattery was entirely beyond him. But to her he was always kind, never once raised his voice in anger, and indeed would sometimes give her a look of great respect.

"I don't deserve you," he used to say, before they were married. "Your goodness, your stability, how *calm* you always are—the way you just get on with things, and make it look so easy . . ."

Respect—that was what she'd taken his words to connote, but might they not in fact have been intended as a confession, that whatever it was he felt for her, it was nothing even remotely resembling love?

Perhaps the only things he truly loved were his images—those he'd filmed, or then again, perhaps only those he had yet to film. The first time she went to one of his exhibitions, after they were married, she was taken aback; she couldn't believe that this man, who had looked as though he might be about to collapse, had carted his camcorder around all these various places, with all the difficulties that must have involved. Indeed, it was hard for her even to imagine how he'd managed to negotiate to be allowed to film in sensitive places, the courage and sheer nerve he must at times have had to display, the patient perseverance that seemed so at odds with everything she knew about him. What it all came down to was that she just couldn't believe he'd been sufficiently passionate about the project to put himself through all that.

There was one time that stuck in her memory. It had been a little after Ji-woo's first birthday, when the boy was just beginning to walk. Her husband had used his camcorder to film Ji-woo tottering around the sunny living room. He'd filmed Ji-woo suddenly being scooped up into her arms, her lips pressed to the crown of the boy's head.

"Every time Ji-woo takes another step," he said, his eyes sparkling with life yet somehow inscrutable, "how about I make an animation so flowers spring up from his footsteps, like in that Hayao Miyazaki film? No, not flowers, butterflies would be better. Ah, in that case we should film it again, on a lawn."

He showed her how to operate the camcorder, played back the scenes he'd just filmed, all while rattling on excitedly about his ideas for the piece.

"You and he'll have to wear white clothes. No, wait, how about if the clothes were really shabby, old and worn? Yes, yes, of course, that's it. A poor mother and child on an outing, the multicolored butterflies that fly up like a miracle every time the baby takes an unsteady step . . ."

But they didn't have a lawn, plus Ji-woo soon grew out of the unsteady tottering phase. The video of butterflies flying up from the child's footsteps never became a reality.

From a certain point onward he began to work himself even harder than before. He shut himself up in the studio, not even coming home in the evenings or at weekends, and yet he never seemed to have anything to show for it. He wandered the streets until his sneakers turned black. Sometimes, when she woke in the early hours and went into the bathroom, she was startled to find him there, curled up in the empty bathtub, still in his clothes, and sound asleep.

After her husband left them, Ji-woo would often ask her, "Is there a dad in our family?" It was the question he'd asked her every morning even when her husband was still around, so infrequently did the boy actually see him.

"No," she would answer shortly. And then, soundlessly: "No one at all. There's only you and me. That will have to be enough, now."

In the rain, the hospital buildings stand dreary and forlorn. Their gray concrete walls appear darker and more solid than usual. The wards on the first and third floors have iron bars over the windows. Many of the patients liked to stick their faces between the bars; on bright days it was difficult to make them out, but with the weather like this several gray faces could be seen staring out at the rain. She glances up briefly, to the windows of Yeong-hye's third-floor ward annex, then walks inside and heads toward reception.

"I've got an appointment to see Dr. Park In-ho."

The receptionist greets her, recognizing her from previous visits. She closes her dripping umbrella and secures the tie around it, then sits down on a long wooden bench. While she waits for the doctor to come down from the consultation room, she turns to look at the zelkova tree that stands in the hospital's front garden. The tree is clearly very old, easily four hundred years. On bright days it would spread its countless branches and let the sunlight scintillate its leaves, seemingly communicating something to her. Today, a day sodden and stupefied with rain, it is reticent, and keeps its thoughts unspoken. The old bark on its lower part is dark as a drenched evening, and the leaves tremble silently on the twigs as the raindrops batter down on them. And she sees her sister's face, flickering like a ghostly afterimage overlaid on the silent scene.

She closes her bloodshot eyes for a long time before opening them again. The tree fills her field of vision, still silent, keeping its own counsel. Still she cannot sleep. It's been three months straight now, three months of getting by snatching pockets of sleep here and there, never more than an hour at any one time. Yeong-hye's voice, the forest with the black rain falling, and her own face with the blood trickling from her eye, shiver the long night into fragments like potsherds.

Usually, when she has given up on trying to wring any more sleep out of the night, it is around three in the morning. She washes her face, brushes her teeth, prepares some side dishes, cleans and tidies every corner of the house, and still the clock goes as slow as ever, the shifting of the hands like the almost comically suspended movements of some ponderous dance. In the end she goes into his room and listens to some of the records he left behind, or puts her hand on her back and spins herself around the room as he once had, or curls up in the bathtub with her clothes on and even feels, for the first time, as though he mightn't have been so incomprehensible after all. He probably just hadn't had the energy to take his clothes off, simple as that. He simply can't have had the energy to adjust the water temperature and take a shower. It struck her that this narrow, concave space was, oddly enough, cozier than anywhere else in the entire apartment.

"When did all of this begin?" she sometimes asked herself in such moments. "No—when did it all begin to fall apart?"

Yeong-hye's increasingly odd behavior had become noticeable around three years ago, when she'd suddenly decided to turn vegetarian. She lost so much weight it was quite shocking to look at her, and she practically stopped sleeping altogether. Yes, she'd always been quiet, but at that time she would say so little that any kind of meaningful communication was impossible. The whole family had been extremely concerned, their parents in particular. All this had happened shortly after In-hye and her husband had moved with Ji-woo to a new apartment. At the housewarming, when the whole family had got together, their father had struck Yeong-hye in the face, held her mouth open and forced a lump of meat inside. In-hye's body had jerked violently, as though she herself were the one receiving the blow. She'd stood and watched, stiff as a ramrod, while Yeong-hye howled like an animal and spat out the meat, then picked up the fruit knife and slit her own wrist.

Wasn't there something she could have done to prevent it? Again and again, doubts raced through her mind. Was there really nothing she could have done to stop their father's hand that day? Or to get the knife out of Yeong-hye's hand before she had time to hurt herself? Couldn't she have prevented her husband from being the one to pick up the bleeding Yeong-hye and rush her to hospital? And then, once Yeong-hye had been admitted to the psychiatric hospital, surely she could have dissuaded her husband, Mr. Cheong, from coldly casting her aside? Above all, that terrible thing that her own husband had done to Yeong-hye, that thing she wanted to put as far from her mind as possible, couldn't she have talked him out of it, found a way to make him change his mind before the whole thing descended into a cheap, tawdry scandal? The lives of all the people around her had tumbled down like a house of cards—was there really nothing else she could have done?

Of course, there'd been no way for her to guess what ideas her casual mention of that small, blue Mongolian mark would spark in her husband. But shouldn't she have been able to at least make a guess as to the way things were heading—hadn't his recent behavior given her sufficient clues? Could she have found a way to impress on him that Yeong-hye was still on medication, was still ill? The only thing clear to her was that what her husband had done was unforgivable.

It wasn't until past noon that first her husband and then Yeong-hye had awakened, followed quickly by the three paramedics rushing into the flat, concealing straitjackets and protective equipment. Two of them had immediately gone over to Yeong-hye, who had been leaning precariously out over the veranda railing. She resisted violently as they tried to slip the straitjacket on over her naked, paint-mottled body, biting their arms savagely and letting out an incomprehensible roar. Despite her struggles, they managed to insert an IV needle into her forearm. While all this was going on, her husband had tried to get around the other paramedic, who was standing by the front door, but the man easily caught hold of him. Using all his strength to tear himself free, he whipped around and, without a moment's pause, ran out onto the veranda. He tried to throw himself over the railing. The quick-footed paramedic got hold of him around the waist just in time, and after that he didn't struggle anymore.

She had stood there, trembling from head to foot, as she watched all this unfold. Eventually, when her husband was being dragged away and their eyes met, she stared at him as hard as she could. But what she saw in his eyes was neither lust nor insanity, regret nor resentment. There was nothing there except the same terror she herself was feeling.

And that was how it all ended. That afternoon, which marked the point after which their lives could never go back to the way they'd been before.

Her husband had been held in a police cell after the hospital confirmed that he wasn't mentally ill. It took several months of tedious lawsuits and official inquiries before he was released, after which he went immediately into hiding—she never saw him again. But Yeong-hye's condition was such that she had to remain in the closed ward. After her initial bout of mental illness she'd returned to the stage where she was able to speak to others, only to now withdraw into silence once more. But it wasn't simply that she didn't engage in conversation; back in the closed ward, she'd taken to squatting down in a sunny spot where she wouldn't be disturbed and muttering incessantly to herself. As before, she refused to eat meat, and if she so much as set eyes on a side dish containing meat she would scream and try to run away. On sunny days she would press herself up against the window, unbutton her hospital gown and bare her breasts to the sun. Their parents, whom the whole sorry saga seemed to have greatly aged, didn't make any further effort to visit Yeong-hye, and even severed contact with their elder daughter, In-hye, who reminded them of the despicable way they'd treated Yeong-hye. The two sisters' younger brother, Yeong-ho, and his wife were no different. But she, In-hye, could not bring herself to abandon Yeong-hye. Someone had to pay the hospital fees, someone had to act as her carer.

And she got by, as she always had done. Despite the scandal

hanging over her, steadfastly refusing to disappear, she made sure that the shop kept running. Time was a wave, almost cruel in its relentlessness as it whisked her life downstream, a life she had to constantly strain to keep from breaking apart. Ji-woo, who had been five that autumn, was now six, and Yeong-hye, who had been transferred to a hospital where the environment was good and the fees were reasonable, looked to have greatly improved.

Even as a child, In-hye had possessed the innate strength of character necessary to make one's own way in life. As a daughter, as an older sister, as a wife and as a mother, as the owner of a shop, even as an underground passenger on the briefest of journeys, she had always done her best. Through the sheer inertia of a life lived in this way, she would have been able to conquer everything, even time. If only Yeong-hye hadn't suddenly disappeared last March. If only she hadn't been discovered in the forest that rainy night. If only all of her symptoms hadn't suddenly got worse.

Preceded by the sound of quick, purposeful footsteps, a young doctor wearing a white gown approaches from the other end of the corridor. He sketches a shallow bow when In-hye stands up to greet him, gesturing toward the consulting room with an expansive sweep of his arm. She follows him inside.

The doctor, who is in his late thirties, has a healthy, robust physique. The set of his jaw and his manner of walking speak of a certain self-confidence; he sits behind the desk and stares over it at her, his brow furrowed. Sensing that the tone of the discussion will not be positive, she feels her heart become heavy.

"My sister . . ."

"We've done our very best, but her condition hasn't improved."

"In that case, today . . ." She blushes as if having committed some embarrassing blunder.

The doctor doesn't wait for her to continue. "Today we'll try feeding her intravenously, and if we're lucky her condition might improve just a little. Otherwise there'll be nothing else for it but to transfer her to one of the critical wards at the general hospital."

"Before that, would it be all right for me to try to talk to her, to make her see sense?" she asks.

His eyes show that he holds no great hopes for her attempts at persuasion. He seems worn out, trying to conceal the anger he feels toward those patients who fail to live up to his expectations. He glances at his watch. "I'll give you around thirty minutes. If you're successful, please let them know in the nurses' room. Otherwise, I'll see you at two."

She expects him to get up immediately and sweep out of the room, but instead he chooses to drag the conversation out a little longer, perhaps mindful of having been a little abrupt. "I know I told you this last time, but fifteen to twenty percent of anorexia nervosa patients will starve to death. Even when they're down to nothing but skin and bone, the subject is still convinced that they've put on weight. There can be all manner of psychological factors at play; a power struggle with a domineering mother, for example . . . but Kim Yeong-hye's is one of those particular cases where the subject refuses to eat while suffering from schizophrenia. We were confident that her schizophrenia wasn't serious; there was honestly no way for us to predict that things would turn out the way they have. In cases where the subject is paranoid about being poisoned, they can usually be reasoned with. Or else the doctor can eat the food in front of them, let them see that it's fine. But we're still not sure exactly why it is that Kim Yeong-hye is refusing to eat, and none of the medicines we've given her seem to have had any effect. It wasn't an easy decision for us to make, but there's no other way. Our first duty as doctors is to preserve life . . . and we simply can't be sure of keeping her alive here." The doctor makes as if to stand up, then hesitates. "Your complexion doesn't look healthy. Are you not sleeping well?" His question seems motivated by professional habit, and she cannot think of a quick answer. "Carers have to look after their own health too, you know."

They exchange bows, then the doctor opens the door and strides away. By the time she leaves the room, his retreating figure is already disappearing down the corridor.

When she returns to the long bench in front of the reception desk, a flashily dressed middle-aged woman is just coming in through the front door, on the arm of a similarly aged man. Have they come to visit a patient? The next instant, an unbroken stream of invective starts pouring forth from the woman's mouth. Seemingly well accustomed to her cursing, the man pays no attention as he gets the medical insurance certificate out of his wallet and slides it under the window at the reception desk.

"Wicked little shits! You won't be satisfied even when you've sucked my insides dry! I'm going to emigrate. I can't spend another day with shits like you!"

If the process of admittance is completed in time, the woman will probably end up spending the night in the secure room. More than likely, her limbs will be bound and a tranquilizer will be administered. In-hye stares at the garish flower-patterned hat worn by this shrieking woman. All of a sudden, she realizes how blasé she's become when it comes to the mentally ill. In fact, after all these visits to the hospital, sometimes it's the tranquil streets filled with so-called "normal" people that end up seeming strange.

She remembers the day she first brought Yeong-hye here. A bright afternoon in early winter. The closed ward of Seoul General Hospital was actually quite near her house, but the admittance fee was more than she could scrape together, so she'd asked around a bit before settling on this hospital, where the treatment was apparently quite good. It was when she'd met with the doctor at the other hospital, who wanted Yeong-hye to be discharged, that she'd been advised to consider outpatient care.

"So far, the results that we've observed directly have been good. She probably isn't in a position yet to return to any kind of social life, but the support of her family will be a great help."

"That's what I was told last time, too," she told him. "I believed it, and had Yeong-hye discharged. But now it seems like that was the wrong thing to do."

Though the ostensible reason for her not wanting Yeong-hye to be discharged, the reason that she gave the doctor, was this worry about a possible relapse, now she was able to admit to herself what had really been going on. She was no longer able to cope with all that her sister reminded her of. She'd been unable to forgive her for soaring alone over a boundary she herself could never bring herself to cross, unable to forgive that magnificent irresponsibility that had enabled Yeong-hye to shuck off social constraints and leave her behind, still a prisoner. And before Yeong-hye had broken those bars, she'd never even known they were there.

Luckily, Yeong-hye was in favor of being admitted. Dressed in everyday clothes and telling the doctor in a distinct voice that she was comfortable there in the hospital, she had seemed calm.

The look in her eyes was clear, and the set of her mouth was firm. It was almost impossible to tell her apart from ordinary people, aside, of course, from the fact that, skinny to begin with, she was at that point alarmingly thin. In the taxi on the way there she'd gazed quietly out of the window, showing not even the slightest hint of unease, and when they sent the taxi away she'd obediently followed her sister as though they'd simply come out for a stroll. She'd looked so normal that the receptionist had actually had to ask which one of them was the patient.

While they waited for Yeong-hye's documents to be processed, In-hye said to her sister, "The air is good here, it'll give you more of an appetite. You'll be able to eat a bit more and put on some weight."

Yeong-hye, who at the time was just beginning to speak again, cast her gaze toward the zelkova tree on the other side of the window and said, "Yes . . . there are big trees here."

Having been called down by the receptionist, a strong-looking middle-aged nurse came and checked through their hospital bag. Underclothes, everyday clothes, slippers, toiletries. He spread the clothes out carefully, going through them one by one, seemingly to check that there weren't any strings or pins. He removed the long, thick woolen belt from the coat In-hye had packed, and asked the two of them to follow him.

The nurse unlocked the door to the six-person ward and led them in. Yeong-hye remained composed as her sister greeted each of the nurses in turn. Eventually, she set the hospital bag down and went over to the window, which had a heavy-looking set of bars running vertically across it. Just then, she was discomfited to find herself struck by a guilty conscience, which she'd so far managed to avoid. Suddenly it was there like a lump in her chest, weighing her down. Yeong-hye walked up soundlessly and stood beside her.

"Ah, you can see the trees from here too."

You will not be weak, In-hye told herself, her lips pressed tightly together. At any rate, she is a burden you cannot bear. No one blames you. You've done well to make it this far.

She didn't look at Yeong-hye as she stood beside her. Instead, she looked down at the bright early-winter sunlight as it splintered over the larches, which had not yet shed all their leaves.

"Sister," Yeong-hye said, her voice low and calm as if intending to comfort her. Yeong-hye's old black sweater gave off the faint scent of mothballs. When In-hye didn't answer, Yeong-hye whispered one more time. "Sister . . . all the trees of the world are like brothers and sisters."

She walks past the second annex and stops in front of the door to the first annex. She sees the patients pressing themselves against the glass door and peering outside. They're probably feeling a bit claustrophobic, the rain having kept them cooped up inside for the past few days. When In-hye presses the bell, a nurse in his late thirties comes out from the nurses' room by the ground-floor lobby, carrying a key.

The nurse closes the door quickly behind him, inserts the key and locks it. In-hye notices a young female patient staring out at her, her cheek pressed against the inside of the locked glass door. Her two empty eyes scrutinize In-hye as though trying to bore through her skin; there was no way she could look at a stranger like that if her mind were sound.

"How is my sister at the moment?" she asks as they climb the stairs to the third floor. The nurse looks back over his shoulder and shakes his head.

"She's stopped talking. She's also been trying to pull the IV needle out, so we had to get her into the secure room and give her a tranquilizer before we could put it back in. How she has the strength to shake us off . . ."

"So she's in the secure room now?"

"No. She woke up a little while ago, so we moved her back to the ward. They told you they're putting the nasal drip in at two, right?"

She follows the nurse into the third-floor lobby. On fine days there are elderly patients sitting on the long bench by the window and soaking up the sun, others engrossed in a game of table tennis, cheery music filtering in from the nurses' room. But today all of that liveliness seems to have been smothered by the incessant rain. Perhaps because the majority of the patients are in their wards, there isn't much going on in the lobby. The table tennis bats lie unused on the table.

She looks down along the ward's western corridor, where, right at the end, the afternoon sunlight shines through the large window more brightly than in any other spot on sunny days. When In-hye came to see Yeong-hye last March, just a few days before the latter disappeared into the rainy woods, Yeong-hye refused to come to the visiting room. When In-hye contacted the head nurse from reception, the nurse said that, oddly enough, Yeong-hye hadn't wanted to leave the ward for several days now. Even during the hour when an unaccompanied walk was permitted, a time that all the patients always looked forward to, she'd kept to the ward. When In-hye asked if she could just go and look at her sister's face, given that she'd come all this way, the nurse came down to reception to accompany her.

When she came upon the unexpected sight of a female patient doing a handstand at the far end of the western corridor, it never even crossed her mind that it might be Yeong-hye. Only when the nurse, with whom she'd just spoken on the telephone, guided her in that direction had she been able to recognize Yeong-hye's long, thick hair. Her sister was upside down and balancing on her hands, her face flushed almost puce.

"She's been at it for thirty minutes already," the nurse said, seeming impatient. "It started two days ago. It's not that she isn't aware of her surroundings, or that she doesn't speak . . . she's different from the other catatonic patients. Up until yesterday we'd been having to force her back into the ward; but no matter what we did she just started up with the handstands again as soon as she was in the ward, so . . . so we can't even force her to stop." Before he went back to the nurses' room, the nurse said, "She'll fall over if you give her a little nudge. Give it a try if you can't get her to talk to you. We would have had to push her over to get her back in the ward, anyway."

Left alone with Yeong-hye, In-hye squatted down and tried to look her sister in the eye. Anyone's face will look different when they're upside down. Yeong-hye's face certainly looked odd, with what little flesh she had on her cheeks pushed down toward her eyes. Those eyes were glittering and sharp as Yeong-hye stared into space. She seemed unaware of her sister's presence.

"Yeong-hye." No reply. "Yeong-hye. What are you doing? Stand up." She reached out a hand to Yeong-hye's flushed cheek. "Stand up, Yeong-hye. Doesn't your head hurt? For goodness' sake, your face is bright red." With nothing else for it, she gave her sister a gentle push. Just as the nurse had said, Yeong-hye immediately tumbled to the floor, and In-hye quickly lifted her head up, supporting her neck as you would with a baby.

"Sister." Yeong-hye's face was wreathed in smiles, her eyes shining as though she'd just woken up from a happy dream. "When did you get here?"

The nurse, who'd been watching the two of them, came up and led them to the meeting room that adjoined the lobby. This, she explained, was where family members could meet with the patients whose symptoms were so severe that it was difficult for them to go down to the visiting room in reception. In-hye guessed that it was also where consultations with the doctor took place.

When In-hye laid the food she'd brought out on the table, Yeong-hye said, "Sister. You don't have to bring that stuff now." She smiled. "I don't need to eat anymore."

"What are you talking about?" In-hye stared at her sister as though she were possessed. It was a long time since she'd seen Yeong-hye's face shining like this; no, in fact, it was the first time. "What on earth were you doing just now?" she asked.

Yeong-hye met her question with another. "Sister, did you know?"

"Know what?"

"I didn't, you see. I thought trees stood up straight . . . I only found out just now. They actually stand with both arms in the earth, all of them. Look, look over there, aren't you surprised?" Yeong-hye sprang up and pointed to the window. "All of them, they're all standing on their heads." Yeong-hye laughed frantically. In-hye remembered moments from their childhood when Yeong-hye's face had worn the same expression as it did now. Those moments when her sister's single-lidded eyes would narrow and turn completely dark, when that innocent laughter would come rushing out of her mouth. "Do you know how I found out? Well, I was in a dream, and I was standing on my head . . . leaves were growing from my body, and roots were sprouting from my hands . . . so I dug down into the earth. On and on . . . I wanted flowers to bloom from my crotch, so I spread my legs; I spread them wide . . ."

Bewildered, In-hye looked across at Yeong-hye's feverish eyes.

"I need to water my body. I don't need this kind of food, sister. I need water."

"Thank you so much for all your trouble," In-hye tells the head nurse. "I really appreciate it." She holds out the rice cakes she's brought and greets the other nurses in turn. While she makes her usual inquiries regarding Yeong-hye's condition, a female patient in her fifties who has mistaken her for a nurse hurries over from the window and gives her a shallow bow.

"My head hurts; please tell the doctor to change my medication."

"I'm not a nurse. I'm here to see my sister." The woman stares deep into In-hye's eyes.

"Please help me . . . my head hurts so much I can't go on. How can I live like this?"

Just then a male patient in his twenties comes and presses himself against In-hye's back. It's a common enough occurrence in the hospital, but it makes her nervous all the same. The patients pay no mind to conventional ideas about personal space, or it being rude to stare at other people. On the one hand, there are many of them whose utterly blank gazes indicate minds shut up in their own private worlds, but then again there are also a certain number who appear so lucid one could easily mistake them for members of the medical staff. Yeong-hye had been one of the latter kind, once.

"Nurse, why on earth doesn't anyone ever do anything about that guy?" a familiar female patient in her thirties shouts at the head nurse, her tone aggressive. "I mean, you know perfectly well how he's always hitting me!" The woman's persecution mania seems to get worse every time In-hye visits.

In-hye bows to the nurses again.

"I'll just go and have a talk with my sister." Judging by the nurses' expressions, they are all well and truly fed up with Yeong-hye. Clearly, none of them is holding out any hope that In-hye's attempts at persuasion will have the slightest effect. She threads her way out carefully between the patients, taking care not to brush against them. She walks down the eastern corridor outside Yeong-hye's ward. The door to the ward is open, and when she enters, a woman with her hair cropped short comes up to her.

"Ah, you're visiting today?"

The woman is Hee-joo, who is receiving treatment for alcoholism and hypomania. Her body is stout but her round eyes give her a sweet look, and her voice is always somewhat hoarse. In this hospital, the patients who are in good control of their faculties look after those with more acute psychological problems, and receive a little pocket money in return; when Yeong-hye had grown difficult to manage, refusing point-blank to eat, she had come under the care of Hee-joo.

"Thanks for all your trouble," In-hye says, and is about to force out a laugh when Hee-joo's slightly damp hand clasps her own.

"What can we do?" Hee-joo says, her round eyes filling with tears. "They're saying Yeong-hye might die."

"How has she been?"

"Just now she vomited some blood. She doesn't eat, so her stomach acid is eating away at her stomach, and she constantly has these convulsions. And now this bleeding too?" Hee-joo grows ever closer to the brink of tears. "When I first began to look after her she wasn't like this . . . perhaps she might have been okay if I'd taken better care of her, do you think? I didn't know she would end up like this. Perhaps this wouldn't be happening to her if I hadn't been put in charge of her."

Hee-joo is working herself up, so In-hye releases her hand and slowly approaches the bed. If only one's eyes weren't visible to others, she thinks. If only one could hide one's eyes from the world.

Yeong-hye is lying very straight on the bed. At first she looks as though she is gazing out of the window, but on closer inspection she actually isn't looking at anything at all. Barely any flesh remains on her face, neck, shoulders and limbs. In-hye notices the hair growing on her sister's cheeks and forearms, fine but unusually long, like the faint down that babies often have. The doctor had explained that this was due to Yeong-hye's hormonal balance being disturbed, something that happens after a long period of starvation.

Is Yeong-hye trying to turn herself back into a preadolescent? She hasn't had her period for a long time now, and now that her weight has dropped below thirty kilos, of course there's nothing left of her breasts. She lies there looking like a freakish overgrown child, devoid of any secondary sexual characteristics.

In-hye lifts up the white bedsheet. She turns the completely unresisting Yeong-hye over and checks that no bedsores have appeared on her coccyx or back. The area that had been inflamed last time still hasn't got any better. In-hye allows her gaze to rest on the clear, pale blue Mongolian mark imprinted in the middle of her buttocks, which are now wasted away to the bone. The image of those flowers, which had spread out from that mark like bleeding ink, covering Yeong-hye's whole body, flickers briefly, dizzyingly, in front of In-hye's eyes.

"Thank you for everything, Hee-joo."

"Every day I wash her with a wet towel, and powder her skin too; it's this damp weather that won't let it heal."

"Thank you so much."

"I used to need one of the nurses to help me give her a bath; now she's so light I can lift her easily on my own. It really is like caring for a baby. Anyway, I was hoping to give her a bath today as well; I heard you're moving her to a different hospital, so this would be the last time . . ." Hee-joo's big eyes turn red again.

"All right, let's give her a bath together in a little while."

"Yes, the hot water comes on at four . . ." Hee-joo wipes her bloodshot eyes, one after the other.

"All right, then I'll see you in a bit."

In-hye nods to Hee-joo as the latter leaves, then covers Yeong-hye back up with the sheet, adjusting it to make sure that her sister's feet aren't sticking out. In-hye checks for burst veins and finds them everywhere; on both hands, the soles of both feet, even her elbows. The only means of providing Yeong-hye with proteins and glucose is the IV, but now there are no undamaged veins left where a needle could be put in. The only other way would be to link the IV to one of the arteries that run over Yeong-hye's shoulders. Yesterday, the doctor phoned In-hye to explain that, as this requires a dangerous surgical operation, Yeong-hye would have to be transferred to the general hospital. They'd tried on numerous occasions to get some gruel into Yeong-hye by inserting a long tube into her nose, but this had always ended in failure as Yeong-hye had simply closed up her gullet. They would try this method one last time, today, but if this too failed then Yeong-hye would no longer be able to remain in their care.

Three months ago, just after Yeong-hye had been found in the forest, when In-hye had arrived at reception on the scheduled visiting day, she'd been told that Yeong-hye's doctor wanted to meet with her. This made her anxious, as she hadn't spoken with him since Yeong-hye had first been admitted.

"We know that it disturbs her psychologically if she sees a side dish containing meat, so we've been taking extra care to make sure this doesn't happen. But now she won't even come down to the lobby at mealtimes, and even if we bring a meal tray up to the ward, she won't eat. It's already been four days. She's started to become dehydrated. And, since she becomes violent every time we try to put in a drip . . . well, I'm not sure we can even give her the medicine properly anymore."

In fact, the doctor doubted whether Yeong-hye had been taking her medication at all. He even blamed himself for not being as vigilant as he should have been, after things had initially seemed to be going well. Just that morning, the nurse had been asked to check that Yeong-hye took her medicine, but apparently Yeong-hye hadn't listened when she'd been told to stick out her tongue. When the nurse then forced her tongue up and used a flashlight to look inside, the tablets were still there.

That day back then, as Yeong-hye lay there in the ward with the drip needle inserted into the back of her hand, In-hye asked her, "Why did you do it? What were you doing in those dark woods? Wasn't it cold? What would you have done if you'd caught something, something serious?" Yeong-hye's face was terribly haggard, and her uncombed hair was matted like seaweed. "You have to eat. I understand you not eating meat if you don't like it, but why won't you eat other things now either?"

Yeong-hye's lips twitched almost imperceptibly. "I'm thirsty," she whispered. "Give me some water." In-hye went and fetched some from the lobby. After she'd had a drink, Yeong-hye let out a shallow sigh and asked, "Did you talk to the doctor, sister?"

"Yes, I did. Why—"

Yeong-hye cut her off. "They say my insides have all atrophied, you know." In-hye was lost for words. Yeong-hye moved her emaciated face closer to her sister. "I'm not an animal anymore, sister," she said, first scanning the empty ward as if about to disclose a momentous secret. "I don't need to eat, not now. I can live without it. All I need is sunlight."

"What are you talking about? Do you really think you've turned into a tree? How could a plant talk? How can you think these things?"

Yeong-hye's eyes shone. A mysterious smile played on her face.

"You're right. Soon now, words and thoughts will all disappear. Soon." Yeong-hye burst into laughter, then sighed. "Very soon. Just a bit longer to wait, sister."

Time passes.

Outside the window, the rain looks to be coming down less heavily than before. The raindrops on the mosquito netting appear undisturbed, so perhaps the rain actually stopped a little while ago.

In-hye sits down in a chair by Yeong-hye's bedside, opens her bag and gets out various containers of different sizes, all tightly sealed. She opens the lid of the smallest container first. A sweet fragrance spreads through the humid air of the ward.

"It's a peach, Yeong-hye. A tinned Hwangdo peach. You like them, remember? You used to insist on buying them even when fresh peaches were in season, just like a child." She carves off a piece of the ripe, yielding fruit with a fork and brings it up to Yeong-hye's nose. "Smell that . . . don't you want to try a bit?" The next container is filled with watermelon, cut up into conveniently sized cubes. "Don't you remember, when you were young, every time I cut a watermelon in half you would come and smell it? With some of them, when we cut them up they gave off this wonderful sweet smell that spread through the whole house."

Yeong-hye remains entirely motionless.

In-hye gently rubs a piece of melon against her sister's lips. She tries to use two of her fingers to part Yeong-hye's lips, but her mouth is shut tight.

"Yeong-hye," In-hye says. Her voice is low. "Answer me, Yeong-hye." She shakes her sister by her stiff shoulders, and resists the temptation to force her mouth open. She wants to yell right into her sister's ear: What are you doing? Are you listening to me? Do you want to die? Do you really want to die? Dazed, she examines the hot anger that is boiling up inside her like spume.

Time passes.

In-hye turns her head and looks out of the window. The rain seems finally to have stopped, but the sky is still overcast, the wet trees still silent. The densely wooded slopes of Mount Ch'ukseong stretch far into the distance. The huge forest blanketing those slopes is as silent as everything else.

She gets a thermos flask out of her bag and pours Chinese quince tea into the stainless steel cup.

"Try some, Yeong-hye. It's infused really well."

She brings it to her own lips first and takes a sip. The taste that lingers on the tip of her tongue is sweet and fragrant. After pouring some of the tea onto a hand towel, she uses it to moisten Yeong-hye's lips. There is no response. "Are you trying to die?" she asks. "You're not, are you? If all you want to do is become a tree, you still have to eat. You have to live." She stops speaking. Her breath catches in her throat. A suspicion that she hasn't wanted to acknowledge has finally raised its head. Might she have been mistaken? Might it be precisely that, death, which Yeong-hye is after, which she has been after from the first?

No, she repeats silently. You're not trying to die.

Before Yeong-hye stopped speaking for good, around a month ago, she had said, "Sister, please let me out of here."

She would often break off mid-sentence, perhaps because she found it difficult to keep talking for a long time, and her speech was mingled with the rasping sound of her breathing.

"People are always telling me to eat . . . I don't like eating; they force me. Last time I threw it up . . . yesterday as soon as I'd eaten they gave me an injection to put me to sleep. Sister, I don't like injections, I really don't like them . . . please let me out. I don't like being here."

In-hye had held Yeong-hye's wasted hand and said, "But you can't even walk properly anymore. It's only now that you've got this IV that you're managing to keep going . . . If you come home, will you eat? If you promise to eat I'll get you discharged." She couldn't fail to notice how the light went out of Yeong-hye's eyes then. "Yeong-hye. Answer me. All you need to do is promise."

Yeong-hye twisted away from her sister. "You're just the same," she whispered, her voice barely audible.

"What are you talking about? I . . ."

"No one can understand me . . . the doctors, the nurses, they're all the same . . . they don't even try to understand . . . they just force me to take medication, and stab me with needles."

Yeong-hye's voice was slow and quiet, but firm.

In-hye couldn't hold herself back any longer. "You!" she yelled. "I'm acting like this because I'm afraid you're going to die!"

Yeong-hye turned her head and stared blankly at In-hye, as though the latter were not her sister but a complete stranger. After a while, the question came.

"Why, is it such a bad thing to die?"

Why, is it such a bad thing to die?

A long time ago, she and Yeong-hye had got lost on a mountain. Yeong-hye, who had been nine at the time, said, "Let's just not go back."

At the time, In-hye hadn't understood what she meant. "What are you talking about? It'll get dark any minute now. We have to hurry up and find the path."

Only after all this time was she able to understand why Yeong-hye had said what she did. Yeong-hye had been the only victim of their father's beatings. Such violence wouldn't have bothered their brother Yeong-ho so much, a boy who went around doling out his own rough justice to the village children. As the eldest

daughter, In-hye had been the one who took over from their exhausted mother and made a broth for her father to wash the liquor
down, and so he'd always taken a certain care in his dealings with
her. Only Yeong-hye, docile and naive, had been unable to deflect
their father's temper or put up any form of resistance. Instead, she
had merely absorbed all her suffering inside her, deep into the
marrow of her bones. Now, with the benefit of hindsight, In-hye
could see that the role that she had adopted back then of the hard-
working, self-sacrificing eldest daughter had been a sign not of
maturity but of cowardice. It had been a survival tactic.

Could I have prevented it? Could I have prevented those un-
imaginable things from sinking so deep inside of Yeong-hye and
holding her in their grip? She saw her sister again, as a child, her
back and shoulders and the back of her head as she stood alone
in front of the main gate at sunset. The two of them had eventually made it down off the mountain, but on the opposite side
from where they'd started. They'd hitched a ride on a power tiller
back to their small town, hurrying along the unfamiliar road as
darkness fell. In-hye had been relieved, but not her sister. Yeong-
hye had said nothing, only stood and watched the flaming poplars
kindled by the evening light.

Had they run away from home that evening, as Yeong-hye had
suggested, would it all have been different?

At the family gathering that day, if she'd been more forceful
when she grabbed their father's arm, before he struck Yeong-hye
in the face, would it all have been different then?

And what about when she first took Yeong-hye to be introduced to her future husband, Mr. Cheong? He'd come across as

somewhat cold; she hadn't taken to him at all. What would have happened if she'd acted on instinct and refused to let the marriage go forward?

There'd been a time when she could spend hours like this, weighing up all the variables that might have contributed to determining Yeong-hye's fate. Of course it was entirely in vain, this act of mentally picking up and counting the paduk stones that had been laid out on the board of her sister's life. More than that, it wasn't even possible. But she couldn't stop her thoughts from running on to her ex-husband.

If only she hadn't married him.

He called her, just once. It was around nine months ago, and close on midnight. Perhaps he'd been calling from somewhere far away, because there was a brief lag after the sound of the coin tumbling.

"I want to see Ji-woo." His oh-so-familiar voice, low and tense—she could tell he was struggling to sound composed—was like a blunt knife stabbing her in the chest. "Couldn't you let me see him, just one time?"

So that was what he'd called to say. Not to say he was sorry. Not to beg for her forgiveness. Only to talk about the child. He didn't even ask whether Yeong-hye was all right.

She'd always known how sensitive he was. A man whose self-esteem was so easily wounded, who quickly became frustrated if the situation didn't go his way. She knew that if she refused him this one more time, it would probably be a very long time before he contacted her again.

Even though she was aware of this, no, *because* she was aware of it, she hung up without answering.

A public telephone booth in the middle of the night. Worn-out sneakers, shabby clothes. A despairing face, no longer young. She shook her head, trying to erase those images from her mind. Whenever she thought of him now, those thoughts were quietly overlaid with the way he'd looked when he tried to throw himself over the railing of Yeong-hye's veranda, trying to fly like a bird. All those scenes of flight he'd included in his videos; and yet, when he needed it most, such flight had proved beyond him.

"I don't know you," she muttered, tightening her grip on the receiver, which she'd hung back in the cradle but was still clutching. "So there's no need for us to forgive each other. Because I don't know you."

When the phone rang again she pulled out the cord. The next morning she connected it up again but, as she'd predicted, he didn't call again.

Time passes.

Now Yeong-hye's eyes are closed. Is she sleeping? Can she smell the fruit her sister put to her lips just now?

In-hye looks at Yeong-hye's prominent cheekbones, her hollow eyes, her sunken cheeks. She feels her sister's ragged breath. She gets up and walks over to the window, where the dark gray of the sky is gradually lightening, the landscape growing brighter at the edges. The light touches upon Mount Ch'ukseong's forest, rekindling its summer colors. The place where Yeong-hye was discovered that night must be somewhere over on that slope.

"I heard something," Yeong-hye had said, lying hooked up to the drip. "I went there because I heard something calling me . . . I don't hear it anymore now . . . I was just standing there waiting."

When In-hye asked, "What were you waiting for?," a fever

came into Yeong-hye's eyes. Her right hand was the one with the needle in it; she reached out with her left and grabbed In-hye's hand. In-hye was shocked by how strong her grip was.

"It melted in the rain . . . it all melted . . . I'd been just about to go down into the earth. There was nothing else for it if I wanted to turn myself upside down again, you see."

Hee-joo's excited tone jolts In-hye out of these memories.

"What can we do about Yeong-hye? They're saying she might die."

To In-hye, Hee-joo's words sounded like the deafening roar of a plane taking off.

There is one memory that In-hye has never been able to tell anyone else about, and probably never will.

April two years ago. The spring of the year when her husband made that video of Yeong-hye. In-hye had bled from her vagina for close on a month, on and off. She'd never been able to understand why, but for some reason every time she washed her blood-soaked pants she would recall the way in which the blood from Yeong-hye's wrist had spurted out into the air. Every day she decided she would go for a medical examination the next day, then when the next day came she would postpone it again. She was afraid of going to the hospital. If it was a serious disease, how much time might she have left? A year. Six months. Or three months. For the first time, she became vividly aware of how much of her life she had spent with her husband. It had been a period of time utterly devoid of happiness and spontaneity. A time that she'd so far managed to get through only by using up every last reserve of perseverance and consideration. All of it self-inflicted.

On the morning when she'd finally mustered the courage to go to the obstetrics and gynecology department, the one where Ji-woo had been born, she'd stood on the open-air platform at Wangsimni Station and waited for the train, which was taking an unusually long time to arrive. Opposite the platform was a row of temporary buildings, their steel structures now decaying, and wild grasses straggling up between the sleepers on the edges over which no trains passed. The feeling that she had never really lived in this world caught her by surprise. It was a fact. She had never lived. Even as a child, as far back as she could remember, she had done nothing but endure. She had believed in her own inherent goodness, her humanity, and lived accordingly, never causing anyone harm. Her devotion to doing things the right way had been unflagging, all her success had depended on it, and she would have gone on like that indefinitely. She didn't understand why, but faced with those decaying buildings and straggling grasses, she was nothing but a child who had never lived.

She'd fought down her feeling of shame and managed to stop trembling before getting up onto the bed. The middle-aged male doctor then pushed a cold abdominal scope deep into her vagina and removed a tongue-like polyp that had been stuck to the vaginal wall. Her body flinched away from the sharp pain.

"So this is why you've been bleeding. Well, it came away cleanly, so the bleeding should start to lessen in a few days, and then stop altogether. Your ovaries are completely fine, so there's nothing for you to worry about there."

There wasn't even a scrap of happiness that she could glean from this. Instead of a serious illness, a possibility that had caused her no end of worry over the past month, it had been nothing but a minor niggle. Back on the platform at Wangsimni, it wasn't only the pain from the operation that caused her legs to tremble. When the train eventually roared into the platform, she staggered behind one of the metal chairs and hid herself, afraid that something inside her would make her throw herself in front of the solid mass of the train.

How to explain the four months or so that followed on from that day? The bleeding continued for around another two weeks, then the cut healed and it stopped. But she felt as though there were still an open wound inside her body. Somehow, it seemed this wound had in fact grown bigger than her, that her whole body was being pulled into its pitch-black maw.

She looked on in silence as spring passed and summer arrived. The outfits sported by her female customers grew progressively shorter, and more colorful. As always, she smiled at the customers, never failed to recommend additional products or give discounts where appropriate, and made sure to pack up a complimentary sample with every purchase. She put up posters advertising new products in carefully chosen locations around the shop, where they would catch the customers' eyes, and handled with ease those occasions when skin-care consultants hadn't got good feedback and therefore had to be replaced. But in the evenings, when she left her employees and walked through the sweltering night streets, brimming with music and crowded with couples on dates, she could feel that gaping black wound still sucking at her, pulling her in. She dragged her sweat-soaked body through the street and away from the crowds.

It had happened around the time when those sweltering summer days had started to cool down a little, at least in the mornings and evenings. When he arrived back at the house early one morning, sneaking in like a thief after several days away, got into bed and tried to put his arms around her, she pushed him away.

"I'm tired . . . I said I'm really tired."

"Just put up with it for a minute," he said.

She remembered how it had been. Those words had run through her semi-conscious mind again and again. Still half asleep, she'd managed to get through it by thinking to herself that it was all right, it would just be this one time, it would be over soon, she could put up with it. The pain and shame had been washed away by the deep, exhausted sleep she slipped into immediately afterward. And yet later, at the breakfast table, she would all of a sudden find herself wanting to stab herself in the eyes with her chopsticks, or pour the boiling water from the kettle over her head.

Once her husband had fallen asleep, the bedroom was still and silent again. She picked up Ji-woo, who had been sleeping on his side, and put him back down so that he was lying on his back, seeing as she did so how pitiful they must appear, mother and child faintly outlined in the darkness.

There was nothing the matter. It was a fact. Everything would be fine as long as she just kept going, just carried on with her life as she always had done. In any case, there was no other way.

She left the bedroom and looked out of the dark blue veranda window. The toys that Ji-woo had been playing with last night, the sofa and the television, the black door flaps underneath the sink and the splotches of grease on the gas range; it was as though she were seeing these things for the first time, walking around the house as though she'd never been there before. A strange pain gripped her chest. It was an oppressive, constricting feeling, as if the walls of the house were slowly closing in.

She opened the wardrobe door and took out the purple cotton T-shirt. Its color had faded, because Ji-woo had liked it when he was nursing and so she'd worn it often in the house. It was the kind of thing she liked to wear when she was ill or just not feeling her best; even though she'd washed it countless times, that milk-and-newborn-baby smell still gave her a sense of security. But this time it didn't work. The pain in her chest got worse. Her breathing grew shallow, and she had to make an effort to try to breathe more deeply.

She sat down on the sofa. Her eyes followed the second hand on the clock as it ticked around, and she made another effort to regulate her breathing. To her surprise, there was still no improvement. A feeling of déjà vu crept up on her then, a feeling of having already experienced this same moment countless times. The proof of her internal pain had been set in front of her as though this were something she'd spent a long time preparing for, as though she'd been waiting for just this moment.

All of this is meaningless.

I can't take it anymore.

I can't go on any longer.

I don't want to.

She took one more look around at the various objects inside the house. They did not belong to her. Just like her life had never belonged to her.

Her life was no more than a ghostly pageant of exhausted endurance, no more real than a television drama. Death, who now stood by her side, was as familiar to her as a family member, missing for a long time but now returned.

She got up, shivering, and went over to the room where the toys had been left scattered. Every evening for the past week, she would take down the mobile which Ji-woo had helped her to decorate, and begin to untie the thick cord. It was wound so tightly that it hurt the tips of her fingers, but she continued patiently until the final knot was untied. She rolled up the colored paper and cellophane, which had been decorated with stars, and tidied it away in a basket, then rolled up the cord and put it in her trouser pocket.

She slipped on a pair of sandals, pushed open the heavy front door and went out. She walked down the five flights of stairs. It was still dark outside. The huge apartment building was illuminated only by the light she herself had left on. She carried on walking, through the gate at the rear of the apartment complex and up the dark, narrow path to the mountain.

The folds of the mountain looked deeper than usual in the blue-black darkness. It was so early that even the old-timers who diligently went out to collect mineral water at dawn were still asleep in their beds. She walked on, head bowed. There was something on her face, sweat or tears, she wasn't sure, and she wiped it away with the back of her hand. The pain feels like a hole swallowing her up, a source of intense fear and yet, at the same time, a strange, quiet peace.

Time passes.

In-hye sits back down. She opens the lid of the last container. She takes hold of Yeong-hye's stiff hand and pulls it toward the plums, running her sister's fingers over their smooth skin. She curls those gaunt fingers around one of the plums, makes her hold it.

Plums are one of the fruits that Yeong-hye used to like. In-hye remembered that, as a child, Yeong-hye would sometimes roll one around inside her mouth for a while without biting into it, saying that she liked the way it felt. But now her sister's hand is limp and unresponsive. Her fingernails have become as thin as paper.

"Yeong-hye." Her voice sounds dry and rasping in the silence of the ward. No answer; she brings her face up close to Yeong-hye's. Just then, though it seems unbelievable, Yeong-hye's eyelids flutter open. "Yeong-hye!" She peers into her sister's empty black pupils, but all that she sees reflected there is her own face. The strength of her own disappointment takes her by surprise, plunging her into despair. "You're actually insane." It's a thought she hasn't been able to countenance these past few days, but now, for the first time, she asks Yeong-hye the question. "Have you really lost your mind?"

An inscrutable fear makes her draw back from her sister, but she remains seated. The stillness of the ward, without even the sound of breathing to break the silence, is like waterlogged cotton wool stopping up her ears.

"Perhaps . . . ," she mutters to herself. "Perhaps it's simpler than I thought." She hesitates, falling silent for a while. "You're crazy, and so . . ." Instead of completing the thought, she reaches out and touches her index finger to her sister's philtrum. A faint breath tickles her finger, warm and regular. Yeong-hye's lips twitch minutely.

This pain and insomnia that, unbeknownst to others, now has In-hye in its grip—might Yeong-hye have passed through this same phase herself, a long time ago and more quickly than most people? Might Yeong-hye's current condition be the natural progression from what her sister has recently been experiencing? Perhaps, at some point, Yeong-hye had simply let fall the slender thread that had kept her connected with everyday life.

During the past insomniac months, In-hye had sometimes felt as though she were living in a state of total chaos. If it hadn't been for Ji-woo—if it hadn't been for the sense of responsibility she felt toward him—perhaps she too might have relinquished her grip on that thread.

The only times when the pain simply, miraculously ceases, are those moments just after she laughs. Something Ji-woo says or does makes her laugh, and then immediately afterward she is left blank, empty even of pain. At such times, the sheer fact of her having laughed seems unbelievable, and makes her laugh again. Admittedly, this laughter always seems more manic than happy, but Ji-woo loves to see it all the same.

"Was this it, Mum? Was this what made you laugh?"

Then Ji-woo will repeat whatever it is he'd just been doing, such as pursing his lips and using his hands to mimic a horn growing out of his forehead, or else making a clattering sound, sticking his head between his legs and calling out "Mum, Mum!" in a silly voice. The more she laughs, the more he ups the ante with his clowning. By the time he finishes he will have run through all the secret mysteries of laughter that human beings have ever understood, mobilizing everything at his disposal. There is no way for him to know how guilty it makes his mother feel, seeing such a young child go to such lengths just to wring a bit of apparent happiness from her, or that her laughter will all eventually run out.

Life is such a strange thing, she thinks, once she has stopped laughing. Even after certain things have happened to them, no matter how awful the experience, people still go on eating and drinking, going to the toilet and washing themselves—living, in other words. And sometimes they even laugh out loud. And they probably have these same thoughts, too, and when they do it must make them cheerlessly recall all the sadness they'd briefly managed to forget.

But lying next to the small, tanned body of her son, after sleep draws itself down over his guiltless young face, the night begins again for her. A time when there is neither sight nor sound of any other living thing. As long as eternity, as bottomless as a swamp. If she curls up in the empty bathtub and closes her eyes, the dark woods close in around her. The dark lines of rain drill into Yeong-hye's body like spears, her skinny bare feet are covered in mud. When In-hye shakes her head to dispel the image, summer trees in broad daylight flicker in front of her eyes like huge green fireworks. Is this because of the hallucination Yeong-hye told her about? The innumerable trees she's seen over the course of all her life, the undulating forests that blanket the continents like a heartless sea, envelop her exhausted body and lift her up. Only fragments of cities, small towns and roads are visible, floating on the roof of the forest like islands or bridges, slowly being swept away somewhere, borne on those warm waves.

There's no way for In-hye to know what on earth those waves are saying. Or what those trees she'd seen at the end of the narrow mountain path, clustered together like green flames in the early-morning half-light, had been saying.

Whatever it was, there had been no warmth in it. Whatever the words were, they hadn't been words of comfort, words that would help her pick herself up. Instead, they were merciless, and the trees that had spoken them were a frighteningly chill form of life. Even when she turned about on the spot and searched in all directions, In-hye hadn't been able to find a tree that would take her life from her. Some of the trees had refused to accept her.

They'd just stood there, stubborn and solemn yet alive as animals, bearing up the weight of their own massive bodies.

Time passes.

In-hye puts the lids back on all of the containers. She packs everything up into her bag, starting with the thermos. She zips the bag closed.

What other dimension might Yeong-hye's soul have passed into, having shrugged off flesh like a snake shedding its skin? In-hye recalled how Yeong-hye had looked when she'd been standing on her hands. Had Yeong-hye mistaken the hospital's concrete floor for the soft earth of the woods? Had her body metamorphosed into a sturdy trunk, with white roots sprouting from her hands and clutching the black soil? Had her legs stretched high up into the air while her arms extended all the way down to the earth's very core, her back stretched taut to support this two-pronged spurt of growth? As the sun's rays soaked down through Yeong-hye's body, had the water that was saturating the soil been drawn up through her cells, eventually to bloom from her crotch as flowers? When Yeong-hye had balanced upside down and stretched out every fiber in her body, had these things been awakened in her soul?

"But seriously," In-hye said out loud. "What the hell?"

"You're dying," she said, louder this time. "You're lying there in that bed, and dying. Nothing else." She presses her lips tightly together, clenching her teeth so savagely the blood shows through, wrestling with the desire to get hold of Yeong-hye's insensible face, to shake her wraithlike body hard and hurl her back down on the bed.

* * *

Now there's no more time left.

In-hye shoulders her bag and pushes back the chair. Walking with a stoop, she hurries out of the ward. When she turns her head, Yeong-hye's body is still rigid and unmoving beneath the sheet. In-hye clenches her teeth even harder. She walks along to the lobby.

A nurse with bobbed hair walks up to the table in the lobby carrying a small white plastic basket, and sits down. In the basket are various nail clippers. The patients line up and each in turn is given a pair of clippers. Each selection takes a long time, as if the patients are trying to decide which pair will suit them best. On the other side of the lobby, a ponytailed nurse's aide cuts the nails of the dementia sufferers.

In-hye stands quietly and observes the scene. Anything sharp or narrow that could be used to pierce or cut, anything with a long cord that could be wrapped around a throat, is forbidden. Partly this is to prevent the patients from harming others, but the main concern is that they would want to harm themselves. In-hye scans their faces, each of them bent over their hands, absorbed in the task of getting their nails cut before their time with the clippers is up. The clock on the wall indicates five minutes past two.

A doctor's white coat flits by the glass door, and the entrance to the lobby opens. It is Yeong-hye's doctor. He turns and locks the door behind him, his movements swift and practiced. No doubt the same could be said at any large hospital, but here, at a psychiatric hospital, the authority of the medical specialist seems even more pronounced. Perhaps it is because the patients here are not free to leave. They flock around the doctor as though they have just discovered their Messiah.

"Just a minute, doctor. Did you call my wife? If you could just tell her that's it okay for me to be discharged . . . here's my wife's number. If you'd just give her a call . . ."

"Doctor, please change my medication. There's this incessant . . . ringing sound in my ears."

"Doctor, won't you speak to him? He's always hitting me, I can't cope anymore. What, now you're at it too? Why are you kicking me? I'm telling you to talk to me."

The doctor gives the woman a relaxed, direct smile, clearly designed to appease.

"When did I kick you? Now hang on, I need you all to talk to me one at a time. When did this ringing in the ears start?" The woman stamps her foot loudly, impatient at having to wait, the feelings contorting her face seeming more like misery and anxiety than violent inclinations.

Just then the door to the lobby opens again and another doctor comes in, one that In-hye hasn't seen before.

"That's the internist," Hee-joo says. In-hye hadn't noticed her arrive. Apparently each psychiatric institution has an internist permanently on hand. This man seems young, though perhaps he just has a young-looking face, and gives the impression of being intelligent but cold. Eventually, Yeong-hye's doctor detaches himself from the gaggle of patients and strides over to In-hye. She takes a step back without realizing it.

"Have you spoken to your sister?"

"From what I could see, it didn't look like she was conscious."

"It might seem that way on the surface, but every single one

of her muscles is tensed. It isn't that she's not conscious, exactly—
rather, it's as if her conscious mind is so completely concentrated
on something, or somewhere, that she isn't aware of her immedi-
ate surroundings. When she's in that state and we force her out
of it, if you saw what happens then you'd know for sure that she'd
been awake the whole time." The doctor seems sincere, and a little
tense. "It can be a difficult thing for a family member to witness.
If we decide that your presence is complicating things, it's best if
you get out of the way quickly."

"I understand," In-hye says. "It's just—"

The doctor cuts her off. "I'm sure everything will work out
fine."

With Yeong-hye's twisting, struggling body slung over his shoulder fireman style, the carer walks down the corridor and into an
empty two-person ward. In-hye waits for the other medical staff
to file in, then follows cautiously. The doctor was right—Yeong-
hye is definitely conscious. In fact, her thrashing is so wild and
rough it's difficult to believe that she's the same woman as the
one who was lying completely immobile only a short while ago. A
barely comprehensible yell erupts from her throat.

"Leave me alone! Leave me alo-o-one!" Two carers and a nurse's
aide grapple with her struggling form, forcing her down onto the
bed. They bind her arms and legs.

"Please step outside," the male nurse says to In-hye as she
stands there hesitating. "It's difficult for family members to watch.
Please go outside."

Yeong-hye instantly turns to In-hye, fixing her with her shining eyes. Her yelling intensifies, and a continuous torrent of words

streams out. Her bound limbs writhe, compelled by some un-
known impulse, as if she were trying to throw herself at In-hye.
In-hye steps forward, closer to her sister, without realizing what
she is doing. Yeong-hye's skinny arms flail about, wasted away to
nothing but bone.

"I . . . don't . . . like it!" For the first time, Yeong-hye enunciates
clearly, though her voice still sounds like the roar of some savage
beast. "I . . . don't . . . like it! I . . . don't . . . like . . . eating!" In-hye
clasps Yeong-hye's contorted cheeks in both hands.

"Yeong-hye. Yeong-hye!" The look in Yeong-hye's eyes as she
shudders with terror claws at In-hye.

"Please go outside. You're only making things more difficult."
The carers grab In-hye by the armpits and lift her up. With no
time to resist, she is pushed through the open door and out into
the corridor. The nurse who had been standing outside takes her
by the arm.

"Please stay here. She'll be calmer without you in there."
Yeong-hye's doctor pulls on a pair of surgical gloves and
spreads an even layer of jelly over the long, slender tube that the
head nurse hands to him. In the meantime, one of the carers is
having to use all his strength to try to hold Yeong-hye's head
still. As soon as they approach her with the tube Yeong-hye's face
flushes crimson and she manages to shake herself free of the carer's
grip. It is just as the nurse had said; impossible to know where
such strength is coming from. In-hye takes a step forward, faintly
dazed, but the nurse grabs her arm and holds her back. Eventually, the carer wrestles Yeong-hye's sunken cheeks back into his
strong grasp, and the doctor inserts the tube into her nose.

"Damn it, it's blocked!" the doctor exclaims. Yeong-hye has
opened her mouth as wide as it will go, thereby managing to close

up her gullet around the uvula so that the tube is pushed out. The internist, who had been waiting to send the thin gruel flowing into the tube through the syringe, furrows his brow. Yeong-hye's doctor removes the tube from her nose.

"Right, let's try one more time. Quicker this time."

Again jelly is rubbed onto the tube. Again the carer pits his robust physique against Yeong-hye's wasted strength, clamping his hands around her head. Again the tube is inserted into Yeong-hye's nose.

"It's in. That's it, now." A quick sigh escapes from the doctor's mouth. The internist's idle hands are busy all of a sudden. He starts to send the gruel through the syringe. The nurse who has been holding In-hye's arm gives her a squeeze and whispers, "It's worked. It's a success. Now she'll be put to sleep. Otherwise she might vomit, you see."

As soon as the head nurse gets out the tranquilizer injection, the nurse's aide gives a sharp scream. In-hye shakes off the other nurse's hand and dashes back into the room.

"Out of the way, all of you! Get away from her!" In-hye grabs Yeong-hye's doctor by the shoulder as he bends over the bed and yanks him back. She stands and looks down at Yeong-hye. The nurse's aide, who had been holding the tube, has blood spatters on her face. The blood is gushing out of the tube, out of Yeong-hye's mouth. The internist takes a step back, still holding the syringe.

"Take it out. Take the tube out, quickly!" In-hye is unaware of the shrill scream coming from her own mouth as she feels the carer try to grapple her away. Meanwhile, Yeong-hye's doctor is finding it difficult to extract the long tube as his patient throws her head about.

"Calm down, calm down! Calm!" the doctor yells at Yeong-hye. "Tranquilizer!" The head nurse tries to hand him the syringe.

"Don't!" In-hye screams, her voice drawn out like a wail. "Stop it! Don't! Please don't!" She bites the arm of the carer holding her and throws herself forward again.

"What the hell, you bitch!" the carer groans. In-hye takes Yeong-hye in her arms, soaking her blouse with the blood her sister has vomited up.

"Stop it, for god's sake. Please stop . . ." In-hye grabs the wrist of the head nurse, the one who is holding the syringe with the tranquilizer, as Yeong-hye quietly convulses against her chest.

Yeong-hye's blood is splashed all over the doctor's white gown, even on his rolled-up sleeves. In-hye stares blankly at the splatter pattern. A whirling galaxy of bloody stars.

"We need to transfer Yeong-hye to the main hospital right away. Please, go to Seoul. They'll have to give her a protein injection into one of her carotid arteries to stop the gastric bleeding. The effect won't last long, but it's the only way if you want to keep her alive."

In-hye takes the letter requesting Yeong-hye's admittance to the main hospital, which has just been drawn up, puts it in her bag and leaves the nurses' room. She heads for the bathroom and manages to make it into one of the cubicles before her legs crumple beneath her and she falls to her knees in front of the toilet. Quietly, she begins to vomit. Milky tea mixed with yellow stomach acid.

"Idiot." Her trembling lips repeat the word as she washes her face in front of the mirror. "Idiot."

It's your body, you can treat it however you please. The only area where you're free to do just as you like. And even that doesn't turn out how you wanted.

When she lifts her head, the face she sees reflected in the mirror is wet. Eyes from which so much blood has spilled in her dreams. Eyes from which that blood always refused to be wiped away, no matter how fiercely she scrubbed at it with her hands. But the woman's face is not crying, not now. It's only staring wordlessly back at her, like always, betraying not even the faintest hint of emotion. The wailing cry that tore at her ears a little while ago was so raw, so full of anguish, she finds it difficult to believe it came from her.

She reels along the corridor, staggering like a drunk. Desperately trying to keep her balance, she makes her way toward the lobby. All of a sudden the sunlight is pouring through the window, brightening the gloomy space. It's been a long time since In-hye has seen such light. Some of the patients are sensitive to the light and grow agitated. While the rest of them flock over to the window, gabbling excitably, a woman wearing ordinary clothes walks over to In-hye. In-hye narrows her eyes, her vision swimming, struggling to make out the woman's face. It's Hee-joo. The whites of her eyes are red; perhaps she's been crying again. Has she always felt things so deeply? Or is it just because she's a patient here, one who's emotionally unstable?

"How is Yeong-hye? If you go now . . ."

In-hye takes hold of the other woman's hand. "I've been really grateful." In-hye finds herself surprised by the impulse to reach out and put her arms around the broad shoulders of this crying woman. But she doesn't act on it; instead, she turns and looks over at the patients who are peering anxiously out of the window. They may be nervous but they're also earnest, captivated, as if longing to walk through the glass and find themselves outside. They're trapped here, In-hye thinks. Just like this woman, Hee-joo. Just like Yeong-hye. Her inability to embrace Hee-joo is bound up with the guilt she feels over having had Yeong-hye incarcerated here.

Rapid footsteps can be heard, coming from the eastern corridor. A moment later two carers appear, taking short, quick steps; they are carrying Yeong-hye on a stretcher. Now cleaned of blood and with her eyes closed, Yeong-hye's face is like that of a baby napping after a bath. Hee-joo reaches out to take Yeong-hye's wasted hand in her own rough palm, and In-hye turns her head so that she won't have to watch.

The summer woods are dense and luxuriant beyond the windshield of the ambulance. In the waning afternoon light, the rain on the leaves glitters intensely, kindling a green fire.

In-hye brushes Yeong-hye's hair, still slightly damp from when the nurse's aide had washed the blood off, back behind her ears. She remembers rubbing soap over her sister's individually protruding vertebrae, all those times when they had bathed together as children, those evenings when she had washed her back and hair for her.

It occurs to her that Yeong-hye's hair now reminds her of Ji-woo's when he was still in swaddling clothes, she feels her son's small fingers brush her eyebrows, and loneliness sweeps over her.

She gets her mobile out of the inner pocket of her bag. It's been off all day; now she switches it on and dials the number of the woman who lives next door.

"Hi, it's Ji-woo's mum . . . I've had to stop by the hospital because of a relative . . . yes, something suddenly . . . no, the bus will be at the main gate at five-fifty, you see . . . yes, it's almost always exactly on time . . . I won't be very late. If I'm late I'll have to take Ji-woo and then go back to the hospital. How can he sleep there? . . . Thank you so much . . . you have my number, right? . . . I'll call again later."

She flips the phone closed and realizes how long it's been since she left Ji-woo in the care of someone else. After her husband left, she'd made it a general rule always to spend evenings and weekends with the child.

She frowns. Drowsiness presses in on her, and she leans against the window. She sits there with her eyes closed and thinks.

Ji-woo will be grown up soon. He'll be able to read on his own, see other people on his own. Somehow or other, he will inevitably get to hear about all that happened, and how on earth will she explain it to him? He is a sensitive child, prone to minor illnesses, but he is also a happy child. How will she make sure he stays this way?

She recalls the sight of those two naked bodies, twined together like jungle creepers. Of course, it had shocked her at the time, and yet oddly enough, the more time went by the less she thought of it as something sexual. Covered with flowers and leaves and twisting green stems, those bodies were so altered it was as though they no longer belonged to human beings. The writhing movements of those bodies made it seem as though they were trying to shuck off the human. What was it that had made him want to film such a thing? Had he staked everything of himself on those strange, desolate images—staked everything, and lost everything?

* * *

"There was this photo of you, Mum, flying about in the wind. I was looking at the sky, okay, and there was a bird, and I heard it say, 'I'm your mum.' And these two hands came out of the bird's body."

This had been a long while back, when Ji-woo's tongue still tripped over certain words. The strange vague sadness of a child near tears had surprised her, she remembers.

"What's all this, hey? Are you saying it was a sad dream?" Still lying down, Ji-woo had rubbed at his eyes with his little fists. "What did the bird look like? What color was it?"

"White . . . yeah, it was pretty." Sucking in a quavering breath, the boy had buried his head in his mother's chest. His sobs desolated her, just like every time he went to great efforts to make her laugh. There was no demand he had that she might fulfill, nor was he trying to ask for help. He was crying simply because he felt sad.

"It must have meant it was a mummy bird," she'd said, hoping to placate him. Ji-woo shook his head, still pressed up against her chest. She slipped a hand under his chin and tilted his head up. "Look, your mum's right here. I haven't changed into a white bird, you see?" His lips wavered into a faint, uncertain smile. His nose was as shiny as a puppy's. "You see, it was just a dream."

But was that really true? Right then, in the ambulance, she wasn't sure. Had it really been just a dream, a mere coincidence? Because that had been the morning when she turned her back on the sun as it rose over the silent trees and retraced her steps back down the mountain, wearing her faded purple T-shirt.

* * *

It's just a dream.

That's what she tells herself, out loud and vehement, every time she recalls how Ji-woo looked at her that day. This time she's startled by her own voice, opens her eyes wide and stares confusedly about her. The ambulance is still racing down the steep road. She smoothes her hair back, knows she should see to it, knows it must look a state. Her hand trembles visibly.

She can't explain, not even to herself, how easy it had been to make the decision to abandon her child. It was a crime, cruel and irresponsible; she would never be able to convince herself otherwise, and so it was also something she would never be able to confess, never be forgiven for. The truth of the matter was something she simply felt, horribly clearly. If her husband and Yeong-hye hadn't smashed through all the boundaries, if everything hadn't splintered apart, then perhaps she was the one who would have broken down, and if she'd let that happen, if she'd let go of the thread, she might never have found it again. In that case, would the blood that Yeong-hye had vomited today have burst from her, In-hye's, chest instead?

With a low moan, Yeong-hye struggles into consciousness. Afraid that she might be going to vomit blood again, In-hye casts around for a hand towel and holds it to her sister's mouth.

"Uh . . . uhn . . ."

Yeong-hye doesn't vomit; instead, she opens her eyes. Her black pupils fix on In-hye. What is stirring behind those eyes? What is she harboring inside her, beyond the reach of her sister's imagination? What terror, what anger, what agony, what hell?

"Yeong-hye?" In-hye says. Her voice is drained of all emotion.

"Uh . . . uhn . . ." Yeong-hye averts her head as though wanting to evade her sister's question, as though the last thing in the world she wants to do right now is to give her any kind of answer. In-hye reaches out a trembling hand, then almost immediately lets it drop.

In-hye presses her lips together. It's come back to her, all of a sudden; the mountain path she walked down, early that morning. The dew that wet her sandals had chilled her otherwise bare feet. There had been no tears, nothing like that, because at the time she hadn't understood. She hadn't understood what that cold moisture had been trying to say, as it drenched her battered body and spread through her dried-up veins. It had simply leached through into her flesh, down to her very bones.

Then In-hye opens her mouth. "What I'm trying to say . . . ," she whispers to Yeong-hye. The ambulance chassis rattles over a hollow in the road. In-hye squeezes Yeong-hye's shoulders. "Perhaps this is all a kind of dream." She bows her head. But then, as though suddenly struck by something, she brings her mouth right up to Yeong-hye's ear and carries on speaking, forming the words carefully, one by one. "I have dreams too, you know. Dreams . . . and I could let myself dissolve into them, let them take me over . . . but surely the dream isn't all there is? We have to wake up at some point, don't we? Because . . . because then . . ."

She raises her head again. The ambulance is rounding the last bend in the road, leaving Mount Ch'ukseong. She sees a black bird flying up toward the dark clouds. The summer sunlight dazzles her eyes, makes them sting, and her gaze cannot follow the bird's flight anymore.

Quietly, she breathes in. The trees by the side of the road are blazing, green fire undulating like the rippling flanks of a massive animal, wild and savage. In-hye stares fiercely at the trees. As if waiting for an answer. As if protesting against something. The look in her eyes is dark and insistent.

Read on for an excerpt from Han Kang's latest novel,

HUMAN ACTS

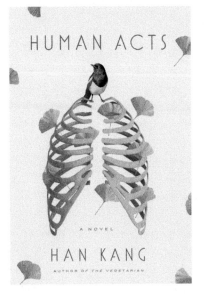

"Remarkable . . . Han prepares us for one of the most
important questions of our times: What is humanity?"
—Eimear McBride, *The Guardian*

"Searing . . . as subtle and specific as it is universally heartbreaking."
—*The Independent*

"A technical and emotional triumph."
—*Sunday Telegraph* (five stars)

The Boy, 1980

L ooks like rain," you mutter to yourself.

What'll we do if it really chucks it down?

You open your eyes so that only a slender chink of light seeps in, and peer at the gingko trees in front of the Provincial Office. As though there, between those branches, the wind is about to take on visible form. As though the raindrops suspended in the air, held breath before the plunge, are on the cusp of trembling down, glittering like jewels.

When you open your eyes properly, the trees' outlines dim and blur. You're going to need glasses before long. This thought gets briefly disturbed by the whooping and applause that breaks out from the direction of the fountain. Perhaps your sight's as bad now as it's going to get, and you'll be able to get away without glasses after all?

"Listen to me if you know what's good for you: come back home, right this minute."

You shake your head, trying to rid yourself of the memory, the anger lacing your brother's voice. From the speakers in front of the fountain comes the clear, crisp voice of the young woman holding the microphone. You can't see the fountain from where you're sitting, on the steps leading up to the municipal gymnasium. You'd have to go around to the right of the building if you wanted to have even a distant view of the memorial service. Instead, you resolve to stay where you are, and simply listen.

"Brothers and sisters, our loved ones are being brought here today from the Red Cross hospital."

The woman then leads the crowd gathered in the square in a chorus of the national anthem. Her voice is soon lost in the multitude, thousands of voices piling up on top of one another, a soaring tower of sound rearing up into the sky. The melody surges to a peak, only to swing down again like a pendulum. The low murmur of your own voice is barely audible.

This morning, when you asked how many dead were being transferred from the Red Cross hospital today, Jin-su's reply was no more elaborate than it needed to be: thirty. While the leaden mass of the anthem's refrain rises and falls, rises and falls, thirty coffins will be lifted down from the truck, one by one. They will be placed in a row next to the twenty-eight that you and Jin-su laid out this morning, the line stretching all the way from the gym to the fountain. Before yesterday evening, twenty-six of the eighty-three coffins hadn't yet been brought out for a group memorial service; yesterday evening this number had grown to twenty-eight, when two families had appeared and each identified a corpse. These were then placed in coffins, with a necessarily hasty and improvised version of the usual rites. After making a note of their names and coffin numbers in your ledger, you added "group memorial service" in parentheses; Jin-su had asked you to make a clear record of which coffins had already gone through the service, to prevent the same ones being brought out twice. You'd wanted to go and watch, just this one time, but he told you to stay at the gym.

"Someone might come looking for a relative while the service is going on. We need someone manning the doors."

The others you've been working with, all of them older than you, have gone to the service. Black ribbons pinned to the left-hand side of their chests, the bereaved who have kept vigil for several nights in front of the coffins now follow them in a slow, stiff procession, moving like scarecrows stuffed with sand or rags. Eun-sook had been hanging back, and when you told her, "It's okay, go with them," her laughter revealed a snaggle-tooth. Whenever an awkward situation forced a nervous laugh from her, that tooth couldn't help but make her look somewhat mischievous.

"I'll just watch the beginning, then, and come right back."

Left on your own, you sit down on the steps that lead up to the gym, resting the ledger, an improvised thing whose cover is a piece of black strawboard bent down the middle, on your knee. The chill from the concrete steps leaches through your thin track-suit bottoms. Your PE jacket is buttoned up to the top, and you keep your arms firmly folded across your chest.

Hibiscus and three thousand ri full of splendid mountains and rivers . . .

You stop singing along with the anthem. That phrase "splendid mountains and rivers" makes you think of the second character in "splendid," "*ryeo*," one of the ones you studied in your Chinese script lessons. It's got an unusually high stroke count; you doubt you could remember how to write it now. Does it mean "mountains and rivers where the flowers are splendid," or "mountains and rivers that are splendid as flowers"? In your mind, the image of the written character becomes overlaid with that of hollyhocks, the kind that grow in your parents' yard, shooting up taller than you in summer. Long, stiff stems, their blossoms unfurling like little scraps of white cloth. You close your eyes to help you picture them more clearly. When you let your eyelids part just the tiniest fraction, the gingko trees in front of the Provincial Office are shaking in the wind. So far, not a single drop of rain has fallen.

The anthem is over, but there seems to be some delay with the coffins. Perhaps there are just too many. The sound of wailing sobs is faintly audible amid the general commotion. The woman holding the microphone suggests they all sing *Arirang* while they wait for the coffins to be got ready.

> *You who abandoned me here*
> *Your feet will pain you before you've gone even ten* ri . . .

When the song subsides, the woman says, "Let us now hold a minute's silence for the deceased." The hubbub of a crowd of thousands dies down as instantaneously as if someone had pressed a mute button, and the silence it leaves in its wake seems shockingly stark. You get to your feet to observe the minute's silence, then walk up the steps to the main doors, one half of which has been left open. You get your surgical mask out from your trouser pocket and put it on.

These candles are no use at all.

You step into the gym hall, fighting down the wave of nausea that hits you with the stench. It's the middle of the day, but the dim interior is more like evening's dusky half-light. The coffins that have already been through the memorial service have been grouped neatly near the door, while at the foot of the large window, each covered with a white cloth, lie the bodies of thirty-two people for whom no relatives have yet arrived to put them in their coffins. Next to each of their heads, a candle wedged into an empty drinks bottle flickers quietly.

You walk farther into the auditorium, toward the row of seven corpses that have been laid out to one side. Whereas the others have their cloths pulled up only to their throats, almost as though they are sleeping, these are all fully covered. Their faces are revealed only occasionally, when someone comes looking for a young girl or a baby. The sight of them is too cruel to be inflicted otherwise.

Even among these, there are differing degrees of horror, the worst being the corpse in the very farthest corner. When you first saw her, she was still recognizably a smallish woman in her late teens or early twenties; now, her decomposing body has bloated to the size of a grown man. Every time you pull back the cloth for someone who has come to find a daughter or younger sister, the sheer rate of decomposition stuns you. Stab wounds slash down from her forehead to her left eye, her cheekbone to her jaw, her left breast to her armpit, gaping gashes where the raw flesh shows through. The right side of her skull has completely caved in, seemingly the work of a club, and the meat of her brain is visible. These open wounds were the first to rot, followed by the many bruises on her battered corpse. Her toes, with their clear pedicure, were initially intact, with no external injuries, but as time passed they swelled up like thick tubers of ginger, turning black in the process. The pleated skirt with its pattern of water droplets, which used to come down to her shins, doesn't even cover her swollen knees now.

You come back to the table by the door to get some new candles from the box, then return to the body in the corner. You light the cloth wicks of the new candle from the melted stub guttering by the corpse. Once the flame catches, you blow out the dying candle and remove it from the glass bottle, then insert the new one in its place, careful not to burn yourself.

Your fingers clutching the still-warm candle stub, you bend down. Fighting the putrid stink, you look deep into the heart of the new flame. Its translucent edges flicker in constant motion, supposedly burning up the smell of death that hangs like a pall in the room. There's something bewitching about the bright orange glow at its heart, its heat evident to the eye. Narrowing your gaze even further, you center in on the tiny blue-tinged core that clasps the wick, its trembling shape recalling that of a heart, or perhaps an apple seed.

You straighten up, unable to stand the smell any longer. Looking around the dim interior, you drag your gaze lingeringly past each candle as it wavers by the side of a corpse, the pupils of quiet eyes.

Suddenly it occurs to you to wonder, when the body dies, what happens to the soul? How long does it linger by the side of its former home?

You give the room a thorough once-over, making sure there are no other candles that need to be changed, and walk toward the door.

When a living person looks at a dead person, mightn't the person's soul also be there by its body's side, looking down at its own face?

Just before you step outside, you turn and look back over your shoulder. There are no souls here. There are only silenced corpses, and that horrific putrid stink.

At first, the bodies had been housed not in the gymnasium, but in the corridor of the complaints department in the Provincial Office. There were two women, both a few years older than you, one wearing a wide-collared school uniform and the other in ordinary clothes. You stared blankly, forgetting for a moment why you'd come, as they wiped the bloodied faces with a damp cloth and struggled to straighten the stiff arms, to force them down by the corpses' sides.

"Can I help you?" the woman in school uniform asked, pulling her mask down below her mouth as she turned to face you. Her round eyes were her best feature, though ever-so-slightly protruding, and her hair was divided into two braids, from which a mass of short, frizzy hairs were escaping. Damp with sweat, her hair was plastered to her forehead and temples.

"I'm looking for a friend," you said, holding out the hand that you'd been using to cover your nose, unused to the stench of blood.

"Did you arrange to meet here?"

"No, he's one of those . . ."

"I see. You can come and have a look, if you like."

You systematically examined the faces and bodies of the twenty-odd people lying against the corridor wall. You had to look closely if you wanted to be sure; your eyes soon started to feel the strain, and you had to keep blinking to try and refocus.

"Not here?" the other woman asked, straightening up. She had the sleeves of her pale green shirt rolled up to the elbows. You'd assumed she was a similar age to the young woman in school uniform; seeing her without the mask on, though, you could see she was older, more like twenty. Her skin was somewhat sallow, and she had a slender, delicate neck. Only the look in her eyes was tough and vigorous. And there was nothing feeble about her voice.

"No."

"Have you tried the mortuary at Jeonnam, and the one at the Red Cross hospital?"

"Yes."

"What about this friend's parents?"

"His mother passed away, and his father works in Daejeon; he lives in our annex with his older sister."

"They still won't put long-distance calls through?"

"No, and I've tried a few times."

"Well, what about your friend's sister?"

"She hasn't been home since Sunday; I came here to look for her, too. One of our neighbors said they saw my friend get hit yesterday, when the soldiers were shooting."

"Mightn't he just have been wounded and admitted to hospital?" the woman in school uniform interjected, without looking up.

You shook your head.

"In that case he would have found a way to call us. He'd know we were worrying about him."

"Come by again tomorrow, and the next couple of days," said the woman in the pale green shirt. "Apparently all the dead will be brought here from now on. They say there's no room left in the morgues."

The woman in school uniform wiped the face of a young man whose throat had been sliced open by a bayonet, his red uvula poking out. She brushed the palm of her hand down over his staring eyes, closing them, rinsed the cloth in a bucket of water, and wrung it out viciously. The water that came out was dark with blood, splattering outside the bucket. The woman in the green shirt stood up.

"How about you give us a hand, if you have time?" she asked. "Just for today. We don't have enough people. It's not difficult . . . you just need to cut up that cloth over there and use it to cover the bodies. And when someone comes looking for a friend, like you did, you uncover them again. The faces are badly injured, so they'll need to get a good look at their bodies and clothes to decide whether it's who they think it is."

From that day on, you became one of the team. Eun-sook, as you'd guessed, was in her final year of high school. Seon-ju, the woman in the green shirt, was a machinist at a dressmaker's on the main shopping street; she'd been left in the lurch when the boss had decided that he and his son, who'd been studying at one of the universities here, should go and stay with a relative outside the city. Both Eun-sook and Seon-ju had gone to give blood at Jeonnam University Hospital after hearing a street broadcast saying that people were dying of blood loss. There, hearing that the Provincial Office, now being run by civilians, was short of hands, and in the confusion of the moment, they'd taken on the task of dealing with the corpses.

In the classroom, where seats were assigned in order of height, you were always the one at the very front—in other words, the shortest. Since March, when you'd started your third year at middle school, you'd finally hit puberty, resulting in a slightly lower voice and a fair-to-middling growth spurt, but you still looked younger than your age. Jin-su's work mostly kept him confined to the briefing room; the first time he saw you, he looked surprised.

"You're a first-year, aren't you? This is no place for you." Jin-su's deeply lidded eyes and long lashes were almost feminine; the university in Seoul he was attending was temporarily closed, so he'd come down to Gwangju.

"No," you told him, "I'm a third-year. And I don't have a problem with the work here."

This wasn't bravado; there was nothing technically difficult about the tasks you'd been assigned. Seon-ju and Eun-sook had already done most of the heavy work, which involved covering plywood or Styrofoam boards with plastic, then lifting the corpses on top of these boards. They also washed the necks and faces with a cloth, ran a comb through the matted hair to tidy it a bit, then wrapped the bodies in plastic in an effort to combat the smell. In the meantime, you made a note in your ledger of gender, approximate age, what clothes they were wearing and what brand of shoes, and assigned each corpse a number. You then wrote the same number on a scrap of paper, pinned it to the corpse's chest, and covered them up to the neck with one of the white cloths. Eun-sook and Seon-ju would then help you pull them over to the wall. Jin-su, who seemed to be permanently rushed off his feet, would come striding up to you several times a day, wanting to transfer the information you'd recorded in your ledger onto posters, to put up at the main entrance to the building. A lot of the people who came looking for someone had either seen those posters themselves or been told about them by someone else. In cases of a positive identification, you would retreat to a respectful distance to wait for the sobbing and wailing to pass. As the corpses had been given only a cursory treatment, it was left to the bereaved to stop their noses and ears with cotton wool and give them a fresh change of clothing. Once they had been thus simply dressed and placed into a coffin, it was your job to oversee the transfer to the gym, and make a note of everything in your ledger.

The one stage in the process that you couldn't quite get your head around was the singing of the national anthem, which took place at a brief, informal memorial service for the bereaved families, after their dead had been formally placed in the coffins. It was also strange to see the Taegukgi, the national flag, being spread over each coffin and tied tightly in place. Why would you sing the national anthem for people who'd been killed by soldiers? Why cover the coffin with the Taegukgi? As though it wasn't the nation itself that had murdered them.

When you cautiously voiced these thoughts, Eun-sook's round eyes grew even larger.

"But the generals are rebels, they seized power unlawfully. You must have seen it: people being beaten and stabbed in broad daylight, and even shot. The ordinary soldiers were following the orders of their superiors. How can you call them the nation?"

You found this confusing, as though it had answered an entirely different question to the one you'd wanted to ask. That afternoon there was a rush of positive identifications, and there ended up being several different shrouding ceremonies going on at the same time, at various places along the corridor. The national anthem rang out like a circular refrain, one verse clashing with another against the constant background of weeping, and you listened with bated breath to the subtle dissonance this created. As though this, finally, might help you understand what the nation really was.

About the Author

HAN KANG was born in 1970 in South Korea. In 1993 she made her literary debut as a poet and was first published as a novelist in 1994. A participant of the Iowa Writers' Workshop, Kang has won the Man Booker International Prize, the Yi Sang Literary Award, the Young Artist Award, and the Manhae Literary Prize. She currently works as a professor in the department of Creative Writing at the Seoul Institute of the Arts.